SISKIYOU COUNTY LIBRARY

3 2871 00430458 6

TO BE CALLED

MA

A Tale of the Lookout Lynching

OFFICIALLY DISCARDED

KATE HILLER

eLectio Publishing

Little Elm, TX

To Be Called Mary: A Tale of the Lookout Lynching
By Kate Hiller

Copyright 2017 by Kate Hiller. All rights reserved.
Cover Design by eLectio Publishing.

ISBN-13: 978-1-63213-432-5
Published by eLectio Publishing, LLC
Little Elm, Texas
http://www.eLectioPublishing.com

5 4 3 2 1 eLP 21 20 19 18 17

The eLectio Publishing creative team is comprised of: Kaitlyn Campbell, Emily Certain, Lori Draft, Court Dudek, Jim Eccles, Sheldon James, and Christine LePorte.

Without limiting the rights under copyright reserved above, no part of this publication may be reproduced, stored in or introduced into a retrieval system, or transmitted, in any form, or by any means (electronic, mechanical, photocopying, recording, or otherwise), without the prior written permission of both the copyright owner and the above publisher of this book.

The scanning, uploading, and distribution of this book via the Internet or via any other means without the permission of the publisher is illegal and punishable by law. Please purchase only authorized electronic editions, and do not participate in or encourage electronic piracy of copyrighted materials. Your support of the author's rights is appreciated.

Publisher's Note
The publisher does not have any control over and does not assume any responsibility for author or third-party websites or their content.

This is a work of fiction. Names, characters, businesses, places, events and incidents are either the products of the author's imagination or used in a fictitious manner. Any resemblance to actual persons, living or dead, or actual events is purely coincidental.

For my desert companions:
Grandma loved it first.
Dad and Mom gave me life on the edge of it.
Jake, Will, and I found imagination there.
Josh, Judge, Kale, and Sarah risk it with me still.

"Some seeds need the crack of freezing darkness
Others seek the warmth of wintered over leaves
Some flowers trust the bee to carry pollen
others risk the wind."

—Linda Hussa

Prologue

I pass my hands over the tops as I weave. Unforgiving branches punish my bare legs for stealing their soft, silvery green leaves. I rub them between my hands, and the scent brings clarity.

"It makes me feel young again, darling. Do you smell it?"

Strength in the absence of nurturing—how could I not find kinship? Sagebrush trampled, windswept, mocked, and overlooked—is there life therein? There is! A taproot has been searching, spreading out below this arid plain toward the source of life. Deep, go wider, deeper! Live so others may, also!

"At what juncture did I choose to live, you ask? No longer the dry bones I was as a young girl or lone tumbleweed? It's never easy to pinpoint the exact moment of resuscitation. And here you are, dear granddaughter, the same age I was at the hotel in Denio, full of questions and yearning for something you can't quite pinpoint. Perhaps, if we sit awhile, here in the desert air, we can unravel my story, the tapestry of my days. Maybe you will be able to see it."

Chapter 1
Dry Bones Live
1910

It could have been in the moment when I was sweeping the porch, a foolish task in the gusty desert of Denio. Afternoon winds were certain in Nevada, but sweeping was the excuse I gave my aunt to stare northwest, toward Oregon. If I listened just right, I'd catch the giggling whispers of my little brother and sisters, whom I hadn't seen in twelve years. *But it's you, Papa, I want to hear! You never finished what you were telling me before Mama ripped me from you—forever.*

I was in these musings, head down, hair whipping about my face, when *he* appeared.

"Want me to spell you awhile? If you're hoping to clear away the dust, it could be a long day."

His words were melodious. I hugged the broom to my side and stood as one turned to stone. A breath finally escaped, and I turned slightly to see through the hair across my face. My ears were not accustomed to such a joyful tone, his words coming as if in slow motion.

"Let go of the broom and let me have a look at you," said the large grin standing across the patio. He made it sound as if he had been sent for me.

I was a stranger to such pleasantries. I'd been helping my aunt run a hotel near the border of Oregon and Nevada for close to three years—without a smile or a "hello" from a patron. Was my imagination going wild? This man had every ounce of his attention on me, and he had the biggest, friendliest smile I'd ever seen. He was laughing as he talked. Each sound awakened in me the realization that I did, in fact, have a beating heart.

"My name is Henry, and I took a room here. I came down to photograph a few of the local families."

I hid in my silence and nodded. I stiffly handed him the broom and broke into a near run toward the door. I almost collided with Aunt Ruth as I rushed in.

"What're you up to now? I asked you an hour ago to start the soup. Were you listening for voices again, you harebrained girl? The pot's on, but the potatoes need peeling."

I was relieved to put some distance between myself and that man, intruder-of-my-solitude. I glanced out the window and saw him standing kind of lopsided with the broom at his side. I didn't know that one could be so long and lanky. It seemed to go hand in hand with his huge grin. I went toward the kitchen and heard the door behind me open with a whoosh.

"Miss, we haven't met properly, and here's your broom."

"Good luck getting a word out of her," my aunt said with a chuckle. "You may as well talk to the broom."

Henry laughed. "I can be patient."

"If Corrie can pull it together, supper should be ready in thirty minutes."

"Yes—Corrie," Henry said my name with a contented calm. He tipped his hat to Aunt Ruth and went to find his room.

Yes—Corrie? I said to myself. He had said my name as if he had already known. *It's actually Mary Cordelia,* I thought smugly. Although nobody had called me that since I left home. That was just as well. There wasn't a single soul alive who knew the real me. The Corrie people saw was just a flighty, awkward girl who stared for long spells out into the desert. Harmless enough, I guess. But Mary Cordelia? That name made me want to crawl out of my skin. Mary

Cordelia was orphaned and hated—by her own mother. Not to mention, an accomplice to murder. Surely that man wouldn't be able to know that about me? That I was unwanted—and a murderer?

I was peeling potatoes as if my life depended on it, save the couple glances I had stolen his way . . . tall . . . vibrant . . . unreal. My senses were under attack. I dumped the potatoes in the soup and turned to escape to our living quarters.

"I hope you added more on account of our guest."

"Yes, Aunt Ruth, but I'm not feeling well. If it's okay, may I stay in the room during supper?" I wasn't lying. It is a strange feeling to have your dry bones begin to take on flesh!

"No, you won't. Henry is pleasant and seems set on getting to know you. Go freshen up and get right back down here."

You don't ignore a lady who runs a hotel in a place like Denio. She was so anxious to be rid of me! She had said that more times than I could count.

"It'd be such a relief to have a young man's help around here. He could do the repairs as well as the few chores you manage to get done—and in half the time, too!"

I plunged my hands into the basin and splashed water over my face. I scrubbed hard as I tried to erase the thoughts waging war in my head.

Who was this man striding into my existence like he was my salvation? My newfound pulse was pounding in my ears. Was this even healthy? Wasn't it too late for me to truly live? This awakening brought back memories I'd hoped were dead. *Lookout . . . the Widow Rawlings . . . Martin . . .*

* * *

I was standing just a stone's throw from the widow's house in Lookout, the bridges being just around the bend. A mist was suspended over the water, shrouding the dangling legs of the men.

"Hush, Corrie, take a breath. It's over. We need to get back before the fire goes out, and we may as well start the day. They're going back to get the old man, and I don't want to be here for that. I've seen enough. There won't be any rest for us tonight and no eternal rest for those forsaken souls. I should punish you for leaving the children and following me here, but it looks like you're already suffering enough with what you just saw."

It was a very harsh glimpse of reality for an eight-year-old girl. I'd let out a scream the moment Martin was pushed off of the bridge. My body could neither move nor remember how to breathe. Mrs. Rawlings gave my arm a stiff tug, and I half walked, half dragged behind her. I tried to look back toward the bridges, but the darkness engulfed me. I imagined the lifeless bodies swaying. They'd be left there until morning.

"I'm so relieved that's over. Now we can all live in peace," Mrs. Rawlings said as she rushed into the house and straight to the stove.

She gave the pot a stir and threw the lid back on with a thud. "The fire's nearly out. Corrie, punch down the dough and get those bread pans ready. When word gets out, our business will surely prosper!"

I carried the heavy bowl from the back of the stove to the table. The spongy mass let out a sigh as I punched down its middle. I let out the breath I felt I'd been holding since the men—and the boy— were thrown from the bridges. I dumped the dough onto the table and started to punch it. Punch and fold, push and fold. With each fold, I tucked in my feelings—no one seemed to care about my feelings. The ones left were pushed away with the others, long forgotten—*joy, affection. That takes care of that, I am all out.* It was a relief that I wouldn't have to bother with those anymore. *Love* was folded neatly back in. *Hope* was the last thing I'd been holding onto. It made me sick the way Mrs. Rawlings had watched them lose their lives and then, in the same half hour, had worried over the cooking. Wasn't there more value to life? Was there something more precious to be found? I guessed not. I was done looking.

"Corrie, if you punch that dough anymore, I doubt it'll ever rise again."

"You're right," I whispered.

* * *

They say memories can resurface decades later without the least bit of warning. In this case, it'd almost been one decade since I'd witnessed the lynchings at the river. Now, as I stood in the room in Denio, with water dripping over the front of my dress, the memory took on fantasy. I longed for my papa to have been there, instead of the widow, taking me in his arms to shield me from the sight of those bodies hanging from the bridges.

"You shouldn't be here, Corrie. Don't look!"

"It's too late, Papa," I said with a sob into his shoulder. "I already saw."

I must have said this out loud because Aunt Ruth gave me another one of her strange glances.

"Corrie! Your dress is soaked, and you haven't even combed out your hair. Henry is already seated, and we need to get the supper out."

She was ripping a comb through my tangled hair.

"Seventeen years old, and I'm grooming you like a child. Just put on a fresh apron over that dress, and we'll have to call it 'Good.'"

She soaked up my tears with a towel and nearly took a layer of skin as well. With a final shove, I was through the doorway and facing Henry.

"Corrie, you're radiant!"

No, you are the one who shines. Henry was, in fact, making a home in my heart.

Don't think me improper, but in that moment, I knew that I wanted this man as my own. I hadn't wanted anything for so long. Just a glance at him kindled my soul. Neither was there anything impure in this man's attentions. It was as if he was born loving me, as if he had been made for me. With one breath rolling its course across the desert, our future was settled.

"Where are you from, Henry?" Aunt Ruth asked between slurps of soup.

"From God's country, up north," Henry answered her with a twinkle in his eye. "I would like to photograph you and your niece tomorrow, if that's okay with you, Mrs. Loren?"

"No *Mrs.* I've never been married," my aunt said stiffly.

"Pardon me, ma'am," Henry said, kindly, of course. He had nothing but goodness in him . . . in his eyes . . . in his smile . . .

"There'll be no charge for the photograph. Won't it be nice to have one hanging in your establishment?"

"That'd be fine," she agreed. "I'll be able to remember Corrie by it."

"Yes," Henry said.

It sounded like everything was agreed! Without a word, he knew I'd be leaving with him. I could barely contain my beating heart or my shaking hands as I went through the pretense of eating. *Somebody finally loved me, wanted me . . .*

"Supper was wonderful," Henry said as he rose from the table.

He walked over and took my hands, helping me to stand. His presence overwhelmed me. My feet were useless, but somehow I was standing as if on air. Then he did something only my papa had done—he gently lifted my chin.

"Let me look at you, Corrie. There's no reason to keep your head down so low. Tomorrow, I'll be photographing the families in the morning light, and I'll be watching for you. There are usually a few others who'll decide to have their photograph done as well. I'll see you then?" His eyes smiled, and he kissed my hand.

I had still not uttered a single word to Henry, but my heart was telling me that this was who Papa had spoken of that dark day at his bedside.

Chapter 2
Hand of the Lord
1898

In my memory, the light was dim and the air stale that afternoon in my childhood home.

"Papa's very sick, Mary Cordelia. You'd better go say goodbye."

Goodbye?

Mama was on her hands and knees, frantically scrubbing the floor as she talked, never giving a moment's pause for me to respond.

"Now, I know this'll be very hard on you. He always treats you like a favorite. Out of all twelve kids, he chose you. I warned him of playing favorites! It never ends well—look at Isaac and Rebekah! I'm sorry, but now that he's sick, I just can't have you underfoot. The others are old enough to bring in money or watch over things while I work. Of course, the babies are too little to send away. You are just sort of stuck in the middle. Remember the widow, Mrs. Rawlings, in California? She knows you're handy enough with cooking and children, and she could really use your help. She never had children of her own, but she took in some young orphans, bless her heart. She serves meals in her town. You can be brave for the family, can't you? Now I'll take you in to see Papa, for just a minute. He tires easily, and we can't have another spell. Don't upset him. You hear? Go on."

Mama thrust me toward the bedroom she and Papa shared. Her hands were cold and wet on my arms, and the door felt unusually heavy as I pushed it open. I watched my feet as I shuffled in. It was dark, a weighty darkness on my small shoulders.

"My little Corrie-girl, is that you? Let me see my girl."

Papa beckoned me with his open hand, the kindest work-worn hand. He pulled me toward him and lifted my chin.

"Mama told me you are going to stay with Mrs. Rawlings down in Lookout." A tear rolled down his cheek.

"Yes, Papa, but I can't leave you." My throat was tight, and my voice didn't sound my own.

"I don't want to be without my little girl, either, but it won't be forever."

"So I'll come back to you when you're better?"

"Yes, we'll be apart for a time, but then together again, Corrie."

It would be some time before anyone else would look me directly in the eye. He had truth in his eyes.

"I love you, Corrie, but let me tell you of One . . .

"Mary Cordelia, it looks like you're upsetting him," Mama interrupted and grabbed my arm. "I told you only a minute."

"No, Mama!" I was breaking up inside as she pulled me from him.

"Corrie, there's One who loves you more than I . . ." Mama yanked me hard, and my hand slipped from Papa's. My sobs filled the house, and Mama carried me out to the shed.

"I'm sorry, Mary Cordelia. I just can't have him suffer another spell. Please stay out here until you can control yourself. I do love you."

Mama gave me an awkward hug, "I'm going to go and pack a few things for you. What an adventure you're going to have in California!"

It was dark before I felt my way back to the house. Mama and Papa's door was shut, and I wasn't to see Papa again. Maybe being his favorite had made me the most dispensable in Mama's eyes.

My folks had lived nearest the community of Haynesville, Oregon for nearly fifteen years. The town's name had been changed to Lorella, but it's hard to change the habits of country people. My papa had moved my mama and my oldest siblings from Arkansas, and Mama had never forgiven him. His dream was to raise cattle in the West, and that is just what he did before he got sick. They eventually had twelve children altogether. Mama's bitterness toward Papa seemed to rub off on the older kids, and it's no wonder Papa did not feel particularly fond of them. They couldn't wait to grow up and move back to the East.

My mama's sour attitude toward my papa's decision to move would come back to get her. I later heard that it didn't take too many years after my papa died for each of them to pick up and move. Not a single one of them cared beans for her or invited her to go with them. You would think she would have had the youngest ones to comfort her. Necessity, however, had caused her to farm the twins out not long after she sent me away. They were living a charmed life in western Oregon. It's to my mama's credit that she left them there to be raised since it seemed they had loving folks. The baby had succumbed to meningitis, and Mama was left all alone. *Alone* is where I'll leave her until a more fitting part of the story.

In all the years of wishing that Papa and Mama had never crossed paths with the widow Mrs. Rawlings, I couldn't deny that their meeting was an interesting story. Papa had never raised cattle before; he'd just read about it in novels. It had been his dream ever since he was a boy, and it must have got into his blood. He loved cattle until the day he died, and by then he was a well-respected cattleman. Land was still up for grabs in that part of the country when he arrived. It was plentiful, in fact—what wasn't plentiful was cattle for sale. After settling in, Papa heard about a bull and several heifers for sale in northern California. By this time, poor Mr. Rawlings was nearing his end, and Mrs. Rawlings was ready to be out of the cattle business. The bull and three heifers were all that was left. Papa left with a single deadbeat saddlehorse to travel down to collect the cattle.

In those days, you were at the mercy of fellow travelers or neighbors to find where someone lived. As Papa neared the Lookout area, formerly Riverside, at Whitley's Ford, he started inquiring as to where to find the almost-widow who was selling the cattle. Maybe the sly chuckles and grins from these informers should have been a warning to my papa. His good nature would never allow suspicion, however, and with the directions to the Rawlings place, he headed there straightaway.

The Rawlings lived in one of the few houses right in Lookout proper. Their house and property were in a terrible state of disrepair, probably an eyesore to the proud people of the town. Young Mr. Rawlings had been kicked in the head by a cow over two years ago, and Mrs. Rawlings was barely making ends meet. (Maybe my papa should have taken note about the kicking cow.) However, he wasn't there for a cow—just a bull and three young heifers. Does that set off a warning to you? Any bull placed with three young heifers will be tempted into mischievous behavior. But, more than that, these Rawlings cattle seemed to possess a fiery gene. An experienced cattleman would know to avoid that gene pool, but my papa was too full of enthusiasm to be deterred. All he could see was that his dream was coming to fruition.

Poor Mrs. Rawlings was a sight to behold, aged way beyond her years. Papa said she had a funny way of fixing her hair—it was sticking out in one direction too many. My papa felt so bad for her that he almost offered to stay around awhile to help.

"I am so sorry, Mr. Loren, but I don't think the bull is here," she said as she twisted her apron nervously. "I can't leave my Charles for more than a few minutes, and I didn't see where he headed."

"That's nothing to worry about, ma'am. I should be able to locate him. You get back in there with Mr. Rawlings, and I'll see what I can do."

Oh, sweet Papa.

My papa nearly knew every soul in Lookout by the time he located that bull. The Rawlings's fences were unfit to contain an animal with such compelling intentions, and the bull had been paying neighborly visits. Mrs. Rawlings surely knew that my papa had been heaven-sent. He made good on his word to find that bull and still buy it after such a hassle. The money from that sale would be enough to see her through her husband's impending death and some months that followed.

Sometimes, I imagined that Mrs. Rawlings chuckled at her good fortune as she watched my papa ride off with his horse and unruly purchase. I imagined those chuckles growing until she was doubled over with laughing. Tears streaming down her face, she probably laughed away all those years of tension. I was glad for her, then.

They say Lookout got its name for the small, rolling hills amid the round open valley. From the hills, Indians could stand watch over any impending trouble. Who had been watching then? No sentry had given warning about what was headed their way. Mrs. Rawlings had enjoyed a bit of reprieve from worries both behind and ahead. It turned out that her cattle were the lucky ones to have gotten out of that country.

But now, back to Papa and his cowboy training... He had the task of keeping his knothead horse moving at a pace to keep up with his half-crazed cattle. The bull had never been in such close proximity to those young beauties before, and he was trying to make an impression. At every homestead along the way, those heifers were frantically trying to seek refuge. In this manner, Papa was introduced to every man between Lookout and Haynesville. I told you my papa was a favorable man, and now he had friends spread across two states. With all those friends, why did they choose Mrs. Rawlings to be my keeper? Perhaps Papa had compassion toward her situation? Or I was sent to be a witness of all that was to come?

Papa was a seasoned cowboy by the time he trotted home to our rough-cut corrals. He had fashioned a long willow switch and was able to keep his herd more controlled. He had even used his lasso a time or two. My brothers said his grin could be seen flashing from an unbelievable distance. He was a cattleman now, and the trip had been a success. That was his optimism for you. My mama could only see the negative side. He had left her alone in that strange country for entirely too long with the children. Now he had come home thinner, with a thinner horse and four rangy cattle. All she saw was more mouths to feed. What she couldn't foresee was the three more mouths there would be to feed in due time. Their cattle business was already growing.

In time, Papa learned that he needed to breed out the craziness from those cattle. The boys had also learned a lot from that first herd and did not suffer for entertainment—but the damage became too much. Kindly neighbors offered to swap bulls. They were looking for a bit more spunk and hardiness in their bloodlines, and then Papa was able to mellow out his herd. As his cattle increased, so did his children. Mama was kept so busy with young'uns she hardly had the breath to complain.

It was in her face, however. Bitterness and childrearing left their mark. Her surly expressions were in stark contrast to the jovial nature of my papa. Why did my siblings choose to take part in her discontent? Isn't it light that beckons the human soul? When I finally came along, my eyes were trained on my papa's goodness. My mama was too preoccupied, at first, to notice my attachment. My older sister was not thriving, and Mama fretted over her while Papa rejoiced in me. His kind hands cradled me, and his smiling eyes searched for me. Nothing tied me to Mama. As soon as I was able, I followed Papa into the bright outdoors, like a string tugged from his heart to mine. The fresh air was exhilarating in contrast to the stifling, sickly indoors. My lazy brothers were usually crowded around the table waiting for food while my sisters fought over the looking glass. If my papa had a fault, it was saving that willow switch for the cattle only. He waited too long in earning the respect of his family.

As I said, it was his light that drew me. There was no doubt he loved me. He would read to me for what seemed like hours under the shade tree, and I would stare out at the pastures and hills beyond. It was our way of escape from the others. I couldn't remember what books he read, but it was his presence I craved—his voice. He also taught me everything about ranching. I grew to love the cattle as much as he did. I did not know that in just a few short years, living as a stranger with the widow Rawlings, these creatures would be my closest companions.

Chapter 3
Carried Me Out
1901

I listened for them before dawn. They beckoned me from the widow's house in Lookout—a welcome escape. First were the faint rustlings, and then their breathing... gentle movements and steady breathing. Their scent, sweet with spring grass. These were the neighbor's cattle, and they were pastured just outside the widow's back gate. Have you seen a cow chew its cud, its eyelids lowered in apparent tranquility? They are at peace who will take the time to draw back up those nutrients to be mulled over again. Those times with the cattle were, likewise, my meditation. I would search deep within my woeful heart to try to understand my situation.

"Why had I been plucked from my home and my papa? My mama never even writes, and it's been years. Is my papa alive?"

I would ask these things out loud. I talked to the cattle. They had time for me, slowly gathering around me where I sat. Surrounding me with their calm and warm, they'd listen.

"Mrs. Rawlings doesn't care for me, and her children probably don't, either. I am only their servant. But you remind me of my papa. He loved his cattle, and they were good to us. He dealt with them patiently, and they kept food on our table. Someday, I'll have a herd of my own. Maybe Papa will be better, and he can help me."

Weeping, I would reach for the face of the closest cow. She trusted me and didn't mind. Her warmth was soothing, and the smell of her green breath made me forget. I stroked her velvety smooth cheeks, and she chewed rhythmically.

"You all need to get out of here somehow. I've been hearing people talk about cattle being stolen, and some cows have even been hurt. Who would want to hurt you? I am so glad nothing has happened to you." I shuddered at the thought.

* * *

These comforting talks with the cattle would come to an end before too long, regardless. Remember? The day was coming when I'd push the last of my feelings into the bread dough. My soul would soon be parched and out of tears. The only one in town who ever seemed to care, besides the cattle, was Martin Wilson. But he would soon be taken from me—silenced forever by a mob of angry men while I watched. Martin had only been thirteen, still a boy. And innocent.

Even in a small town, it was hard to keep Martin's family straight. His family tree was as twisted as an old juniper. There were the Wilsons and the Halls, Martin being both. Martin was a full-blooded Indian, as was his sister Agnes, only a year younger than he. They were the only true Wilson kids. Martin had countless Hall half-siblings who were mostly half-white. Frank was the only other full-blooded Indian boy in the family. Don't ask me how that happened! Frank was also full-blooded evil. All the kids in town kept clear of him. Martin wasn't that way at all, though—he was thoughtful and kind. He would often stop by the widow Rawlings's to see if she needed firewood cut. I wonder if he was as thoughtful to his own mother. I can't imagine anyone wanting to do her a favor.

His mama, Mary Hall, known by some as Mary Joe, was a Pit River Indian. I often thought she should have hung from the bridge. There was even a noose fashioned for her. In my mind, all the fault lay with her. I was very thankful that none of the kids in Lookout knew that my real name was Mary. I would never want to be compared to her. A "woman of many loves" wrote Colonel Thompson in his *Reminiscences of a Pioneer*. Mary Hall had brought destruction with each man she loved and each child she bore. It seems that the first man in her life was a Captain Wagner who was stationed at Fort Crook. She'd been just a teenager at the time. I think her oldest son, Frank, grew up hearing these stories of his mother's shameful love life, and it fueled his bitterness and anger.

You really can't fault him for feeling that way. The situation only grew more sordid. How would you feel to hear that your mama had been pawned off by Captain Wagner on another white man with the bribe of a portable sawmill? That was just what happened. The captain's commission was over, and he quickly passed Mary off to a soldier named Calvin Hall. I believe Mr. Hall would have taken Mary without the sawmill, but of course he wasn't going to turn it down. Mr. Hall had come west from Ohio for the Gold Rush before joining the California Cavalry. He was demoted once for drunkenness but was otherwise respected. In 1864, he had mustered out, and that sawmill might've sounded like a good way to bring in some revenue. Calvin and Mary started their life together out in Gouger Neck. Calvin, a handsome enough man with light eyes and a full beard, became a well-liked man in the community. Mary didn't appreciate Calvin's attentions being anywhere but with her, and the harder he worked, the more she thought of wandering. So, wander she did, and she didn't seem to have trouble finding other men. This took the spark out of Calvin Hall.

I don't know the hold that Mary had over all these men, but the men were countless. On the outside, she tried to fit the picture of a respectable housewife to her loyal Calvin. Sweet Mary Joe, her hair done up in an intricate style and her dress proper. She could be seen carrying a basket of eggs, vegetables, or handwork to sell. This was all just a cover-up for her busybody ways. Going house to house to peddle her wares was a path to destruction. Mr. Hall should've kept her busy at home. Children were born at a steady pace, but it's difficult to track which children she had with whom. James seems to have been Calvin Hall's natural son, and he was born around 1881. About four years later, near the time she finally divorced Calvin Hall and deserted James, she ran off for a very brief union to a fellow Indian—one of Calvin's hired hands. This would be Martin's father, Mr. Wilson. He was apparently a loving father to Martin.

And everyone knows that a father's love makes all the difference.

Martin kept his father's name, while the older boys, James and Frank, had the Hall name. The people in town had long ago lost track of how many daughters Mary had. I know for certain there were at least Mary Nevada, Dora Daisy and Martin's full sister Agnes. There may have been one or two more. Like Martin, Agnes was dearly loved by her real father. The other daughters had been scattered and were being raised by various people in the community. Take note here, with all those children, Mary played favorites with Frank. All the others seemed to pale in comparison. Did that devotion make Frank a better person? No, the opposite was true. Frank grew into a hard and resentful young man, even toward his own tribe. He stuck close to his mother, though, and ultimately, his dark nature must have fallen from her tree.

The whole situation was cursed. It was very uncommon in those days to commit that much public infidelity. The women in Lookout and Big Valley watched it all unfold with horror. At the same time, their disgust and hatred for Mary grew. They kept a tight hold on their husbands and sons. I wonder if Calvin Hall began to regret the burden that he chose to bear by taking on Mary and her brood? Did he regret relinquishing his backbone? The faithfulness he showered on his mixed family would be his downfall. As little as they thought of Calvin, they took every opportunity to take advantage of him. Long after the divorce, Mary and Frank could be found squatting at Calvin's farm.

Frank's wicked nature was fueled by the hateful eyes of the townspeople. Frank grew into a big man, and one capable of great harm. He gradually poisoned the heart of his younger half-brother James, or Jim they called him. Frank knew Calvin Hall was a weak man, and he let Jim know. Soon Jim was in full rebellion and idolizing his strong, older brother. Jim was willing to do whatever Frank asked, and the Hall Gang began to take shape.

On the outskirts of Lookout, there was a wealthy rancher named Mr. Heins. He was known to hire the Indian men to help during his hay harvest. He was well-liked and doted on his family. He had bought a splendid saddlehorse for his wife, and Mrs. Heins would ride it to town from time to time to visit a sister. Her gelding, Pal, was very popular with the children. Mrs. Heins would allow the children to dote on him while he was hitched outside her sister's house. The children would pet him until he shone, and he would nicker with contentment. I was only an observer to this frolicking-of-playmates. *Playfulness* had stayed behind when I had to leave the twins and the baby. Sometimes, I would hope for the Hall Gang to walk by. Then the children would scatter, and I could have Pal to myself.

* * *

Was my *hoping* to blame for what happened next? One day, the Hall boys did walk by, sneering and pointing. The children scattered like chicks, terrified. Frank and Jim saw Pal hitched there and stopped to gaze at him. They looked disgusted, whispering to each other and spitting. You see, Frank and Jim did not like Mr. Heins. He had hired some Modoc Indians for the harvest—but not Frank and Jim. They had inquired about the job but were not chosen because of their mother. The Hall boys had made up their minds for revenge. I watched with a knot in my stomach as they approached Pal and grabbed his tail. They gave it a tug, laughed and walked away. Pal was good natured and only gave a slight, warning kick.

I looked around to see if anyone else was looking then ran to comfort Pal and to get a turn at his glossy coat. Apparently, Mrs. Heins and her sister were too engrossed in conversation to take notice of him. I let my hand slide over his neck and shoulder and spoke soothingly to him. I pressed my cheek against his and breathed in his warm, dusty smell. I was disturbed. The Hall boys had given me a horrible feeling. I loosened Pal's rope just enough that he could get away if he wanted.

"You should run, Pal. *Get away from here*. I don't like the way they were looking at you. Please run!"

I heard a friendly chuckle behind me and turned to see Martin Wilson approach.

"Looks like you found a friend, Corrie. Isn't he splendid? They must give him one of those fancy feeds. Have you seen Frank and

Jim? Mr. Hall is looking for them. I don't know why he puts up with them. I think he should give them the toe of his boot."

I liked having him there, like a kind, older brother. He stood opposite me with Pal's head between us. We stood in silence for a while, stroking him gently. Martin's eyes, tired and worried, would meet mine occasionally, and his hand brushed mine. He was whispering to Pal, but I couldn't hear what he was saying. At one point, he covered my hand with his and held it. His look was grave.

"Corrie, I don't want you walking alone out here anymore. It isn't safe. I couldn't bear it if something happened to you." His voice, deeper than I remember, cracked. "You're special. I see a light burning in you that none of the other girls have. Use it for good, Corrie."

I didn't know what to say, so I didn't say anything. I wished I would have answered him, so he would have known I cared. Martin moved around Pal and reached over me to fix the lead rope. He lingered there for a moment. He smelled like the crisp dawn. That refreshing smell when I would burst outside with Papa at first light.

Beloved.

"There," he said, double checking the rope. "We wouldn't want this prize animal getting away now, would we?"

If only Pal and Martin would have run free then, leaving all ropes behind.

He roughed up my hair a little and walked off in the direction of his half-brothers. I watched him walk away, and he looked sad, just a boy carrying the weight of a man. *Wait, Martin . . . I think I love you . . .*

Yes, it was love I was feeling for him. He was kind and steady, honest and true, like my papa. It was a shock. It had been a while since I'd felt that feeling. It's always a surprise though, isn't it, when love comes along? Like that day, years later, in Nevada, with Henry.

Chapter 4
Spirit of the Lord
1910

"You turned into a woman when I wasn't looking, Corrie," Aunt Ruth said in Denio as she rifled, huffing and puffing, through the trunks for something decent to wear. "If I would've had some warning, I might've taken more care with our clothes. This picture-making and Henry appeared out of nowhere!"

It was true. He had blown south across the desert without a whisper of warning. You would think if something so miraculous was about to happen, I would have sensed it. But miracles are unexpected, like when the arrowleaf flowers spring forth in the desert. The animals have had their share of winterfat, or white sage, through the endless, bleak, cold days of winter—life ebbing away. Without a warning, the yellow flowers burst open, and the large and small animals find their salvation! *We will live*!

* * *

First a servant to Mrs. Rawlings, and then to Aunt Ruth, I had met the needs of others for close to twelve years. I try not to find too much fault in either the widow or Aunt Ruth. They were decent enough to me but ignorant of affection. After nine years with Mrs. Rawlings, she had shooed me away with just a "Go on now, girl" to a life in a foreign land. I was dispatched just as quickly as the ones hanging from the bridges. She no longer needed my help, as her children weren't the namby-pambies I'd expected them to be. They had, in fact, matured into somewhat useful humans. I do give myself some credit for this. I had not allowed them much laziness or caterwauling. Perhaps Mrs. Rawlings could finally sit back a little after so many rough years.

The excuse the widow gave for my send-off was that she'd caught wind of my Aunt Ruth taking over a hotel near the Oregon and Nevada border.

* * *

"Oh, that poor woman, your aunt. She's no idea the strange waters she's about to enter. She's your papa's sister, though, and you'll be a comfort to her. It'd be good for you to be back with your own kin."

By that time, we had gotten word that my papa had, in fact, died, only weeks after Mama sent me away. It was as if our hearts shared something vital that was severed at our separation, and we began to bleed out. My time must also be getting near. Remember how I'd lost all remaining hope the morning of Martin's murder? I was losing strength--no different than Mrs. Rawlings's withering, drooping hollyhocks. It sounded as if the widow was shipping me off to a forsaken wilderness—and the quicker, the better.

Mrs. Rawlings made inquiries and learned that wagons frequented Alturas, California, a town about fifty miles from Lookout, and the seat of Modoc County. From there, a wagon would sometimes go the hundred or more miles to Denio Station, Nevada. Increasing numbers of settlers had worked their way from Winnemucca, Nevada into Oregon. A few—perhaps the crazy ones—had stopped and made homes on ranches throughout the valleys in between. This *Nevada* didn't sound like a desirable place— more like a wasteland. The widow was hoping I could catch the rare supply wagon headed east into Nevada. She was banking on that slim chance and didn't seem overly concerned about the Indian activity that still threatened. Wasn't being sent east considered to be a curse?

Cain went out from the presence of the LORD, and dwelt in the land of Nod, on the east of Eden.

How did I recall those words? Something told me that Cain wasn't a favorable character, heading out from the presence of the Lord and all. Here I was, being banished to the East, just as he'd been. That was also the direction of the bridges where the hangings were. The bridges were only spitting distance from town, but I did everything possible to avoid them.

Mrs. Rawlings made contact with Mr. Heins and asked if she could send me along to Alturas the next time he went there for business. Mr. Heins had only grown kinder with each passing year and was always looking for ways to spread his generosity.

"I'd be happy to escort Miss Corrie, ma'am. In fact, I'll be headed to Alturas in a fortnight. But are you sure you want to send her through that rough country beyond there? I heard talk not too long ago of a sheepherder being killed somewhere in those badlands."

Mr. Heins was looking at Mrs. Rawlings as if questioning her sanity. He was either pondering her decision or, perhaps, the unique way she fixed her hair.

"Corrie's a tough one, remember. I'm sending her to her father's sister. I think she will hold her own if needed. She'll be ready in a fortnight, and I'm most obliged." With that, she shut the door on Mr. Heins.

I was packed in a matter of minutes as I had little in the way of earthly belongings. One of the widow's customers had given me a pretty case with cosmetic powder and a mirror. Mrs. Rawlings let me keep the worn book of rhymes I'd often read to her children. I had a couple of handkerchiefs. These were my only treasures. I had nothing left from Haynesville, having outgrown all the clothes from Mama long ago.

The fortnight passed without much fanfare. I'd catch the children staring at me with what may have been suspicion or awe. They had probably already imagined the bloody fate I might meet at the hands of murderous savages. The daughter, Mildred, broke away from Mrs. Rawlings at the last minute to cling to me. She choked back sobs and begged for me to stay.

"I don't want you to leave, Corrie. Who'll read to me? I'll miss you."

A knot formed in my throat, but if you remember correctly, I was clean out of tears. I patted her on the back and removed a pressed handkerchief from my cardboard case.

"Here, Mildred, you keep this. You are getting to be so grown up. You're a fine reader, and you won't need me."

I gave her an awkward pat and turned to the horse Mr. Heins had waiting for me. The horse was saddled with his wife's sidesaddle, and sitting on it, I felt surprisingly refined. For a moment, I fancied I was Mrs. Heins, forgetting my threadbare clothes and disheveled hair. I climbed up and looked down at Mrs. Rawlings and her small clan. I was curious how I would be dismissed after these long years of side-by-side existence.

"I trust you'll find her safe passage, Mr. Heins. All right then, go on now, girl."

I got one last glimpse of her untidy hair waving in the wind as she turned and snatched hold of Mildred's arm. I could still feel those fingers on my own arm as she had torn me away from the sight of Martin swaying from the rope. Though six years had passed, the chill of that dark morning returned with the memory.

Mr. Heins and I soon reached the main bridge spanning the width of the Pit River, with the small one over the slough nearby. I was nauseous, my icy hands clutching the reins as my mount slowly made his way over. His hooves made a deep, thudding noise that I could feel. It was as if I was hearing the footsteps of the vigilantes and the accused in those predawn hours.

At first, I had only followed the sounds that dark morning, but then it was the torches that beckoned me to go all the way. The men hadn't tied the feet of the Hall Gang. I'm guessing they didn't want to have to drag them the distance. They'd tied only their hands. I stifled a sob into my sleeve so Mr. Heins wouldn't notice. I couldn't look down or I knew I'd faint headlong into the river. Why hadn't I spoken up that moment before they took Martin's life? Maybe I could've stopped them. I'd been a coward, struck dumb, unable to utter a sound until it was too late.

Mr. Heins did not seem in a rush that day as he led me away from Lookout toward Alturas in the northeast. He had a passion for the land around us and its history. The snow-covered slopes of Mt. Shasta towered above and behind us as the valley opened up. My neck grew sore with my bobbing head as I strained to watch it as long as possible.

Mr. Heins must have noticed the object of my wonderment and quoted:

> Stern constancy with stars, to keep
> Eternal watch while eons sleep;
> To tower proudly up and touch
> God's purple garment-hems that sweep
> The cold blue north! Oh, this were much!

"Joaquin Miller spent a lot of time around the local Indians, was even shot by one, and he penned that about Mt. Shasta."

The whole experience put me in a trance, as did the tale Mr. Heins soon wove of loyalty and bravado. I was comforted by his voice and able to remove thoughts of bridges and ropes for the time being. Though the Indians in his story had done their share of wrongs against the whites, I couldn't help but notice the admiration in his voice, particularly for an Indian called Captain Jack.

Not too long before Papa and Mama were settling into Haynesville, there had been a life and death campaign almost directly south of there in California. Kintpuash, named Captain Jack by traders, was a Modoc chief, and his tribe had been in various conflicts with white settlers for decades. His father, a Modoc chief, had even been killed by whites. Mr. Heins told the tale of a horrific massacre purportedly carried out by the Modocs at a place now called Bloody Point, on the shores of Tule Lake. Up to eighty settlers, including women and children, may have been killed. The horror was unimaginable, with the Indians using steel arrowheads. Two girls were even kidnapped and killed later by envious Modoc women. I was not feeling very fond of these Modocs, and my next question was if Mary Hall was actually a Modoc Indian.

"No, Corrie, she isn't. Captain Jack did have a sister named Mary, oddly enough. They called her Queen Mary, and she was said to be quite beautiful. Queen Mary had a lot of influence with her brother. But, you see, Mary Hall is a Pit River Indian, through and through," Mr. Heins said with melancholy.

I was surprised when Mr. Heins let out a soft chuckle. "Now, that's a lot of Marys. Mrs. Rawlings told me that your real name is Mary, too. I haven't heard of that many Marys since I read the book of John. Did you know there were three Marys at the cross with Jesus?"

I numbly shook my head, and my insides hurt. My face must have betrayed my turmoil.

"Now Corrie, don't hold any grudges toward Mary Hall. We'll never know that whole story this side of heaven. Did you know that Frank wasn't even her biological child? I heard she had adopted him as a baby and raised him. Frank's birth mother had been a wild drunk, abused by men. We need to give Mary some credit for taking him on. We must not be their judge. Only the Almighty can take on that task."

I couldn't understand how Mr. Heins could forgive a family who brought so much destruction on others, as well as themselves. Mr. Heins must simply be perfect and thus a far better person than I.

"I have hired Modoc Indians to work on my place from time to time, and that's how I learned about Captain Jack and his intent to restore his people to their lands. Corrie, I do think our Creator intended lands for the use of particular people and not for others. Look how He designated the Promised Land for his special people. How can any mortal decide what is truly theirs? I think they must know it in their hearts. It has to be born out of a contentment of the soul, not of greed. There must also be a spirit of generosity and good will. I don't think it was in that spirit that the Modocs were forced to move off their lands. Who could fault them for taxing the settlers who moved into the area? Isn't that the way of the world? But as I said, I cannot judge the human heart, and the Indians had likewise committed their share of atrocities. A man named Hooker Jim was particularly vile. Captain Jack had compared him to a coyote. The admirable part of the story is the stand that Captain Jack took with his people to do what he believed was right."

Mr. Heins went on to tell how Captain Jack and his people had been coerced into living on a reservation, apparently not receiving what the government had promised. Their food and supplies weren't adequate, and Captain Jack felt his people would be much better off hunting as they had for generations. They had also been required to live side by side with an enemy tribe, the Klamaths, who were treated more favorably. Captain Jack, as protector of his tribe, made the decision to move his people off to give them a better life.

This all came to a head when a group of US troops, citizens, and militia came by dark to force the tribe back onto the reservation. All was going peaceably until a skirmish broke out between an Indian named Scarface Charley and a member of the cavalry. Captain Jack said it would've gone better if they had been approached face-to-face as men, not by cowards under the cover of darkness. The Indians fought, getting back their forfeited weapons, and made off toward a section of California that sounds like hell cooled off. It is called a lava bed as it must have been flowing thick with lava at one time. Once cooled, it became an uninhabitable maze of fissures, caves, and outcroppings. The Indians decided this would be a safe place to hide—a courageous plan. They piled up rocks in places where they would need extra defense. But some renegades showed up days later, bringing trouble. Captain Jack's loyalty to them, particularly Hooker Jim, may have been his downfall.

Like Mr. Hall, protecting Mary and her rabble-rousers.

The whites must have been tenderfooted in the winter conditions as they had held back from pursuing the Indians for well over a month. Finally, hundreds of whites, along with a handful of Indian scouts, made their way to the lava beds. From afar, they saw just a flat piece of land, and they were not deterred. I bet they were surprised when they got close! It probably would've been humorous watching them try to navigate through that rock-hard mess. There isn't an even piece of ground anywhere, and every step was precarious. The Modocs were easily able to pick them off, one by one, and stay put in their rough hideout.

Captain Jack, once a known friend of whites, was in anguish over the situation. He desired peace. Various meetings to work out an agreement only confused matters, especially with Hooker Jim in the mix. Captain Jack pleaded for a home on Lost River for his people, but he would have to give up Hooker Jim in return. Captain Jack was not willing to turn against Hooker Jim.

With threats, Hooker Jim demanded Captain Jack kill the general, Edward Canby. Many others took up this plea as well. On Good Friday, 1873, when the meeting between Canby and Captain Jack did not go well, Captain Jack did as his people wished. General Canby was dead.

More serious attempts were soon made to capture the Modocs, but their hideout was genius. However, by then, Hooker Jim had turned against Captain Jack, becoming a traitorous "Modoc Bloodhound." He had agreed to help track down Captain Jack. Once again, this was not easy in that unforgiving lava bed, every step uncertain—one fall could impale you! When all was said and done, just over a hundred natives were able to hold off close to a thousand pursuers for over half a year. The Indians were eventually caught, and Captain Jack surrendered, ceremoniously laying down his rifle. He was hanged with three others. Hooker Jim died later as a coward in Oklahoma.

"The hired hands told me some of Captain Jack's own words. As a boy, he wanted to be a friend to whites, but as time went on, he grew bitter against them. He said his own people had talked him into shooting General Canby, which was his fatal mistake. Captain Jack wondered if whites ever got punished for killing Indians—an insightful question. He didn't want to die with a rope around his neck and would've preferred dying on a battlefield. They say

Captain Jack was courageous as he met his fate in the end, though—what a sad affair."

I tensed up at the mention of hangings and closed my ears to Mr. Heins. Despite his wrongdoings, I had liked hearing about Captain Jack. Mr. Heins said he'd been very handsome and, also, heroic for standing up for his people and beliefs. Hooker Jim had been the true scoundrel, murdering white settlers and then betraying Captain Jack. Captain Jack reminded me of my handsome Martin, a guardian of his loved ones.

Of me.

Tears made their way down my cheek, and I quickly wiped them away. Hooker Jim and Mary Hall would have done well together, and I hated them both. If I had any softness left in my heart, I couldn't feel it. My heart was dry and cracked, probably a lot like Captain Jack's black, hardened lava hideout.

We reached the town of Canby, which was named for the murdered general that Mr. Heins had just told me about. There was a wayside inn there. Mr. Heins said we would stop there for the night and to have a bite to eat. We hitched the horses outside and entered the dim saloon and dining area. I had never been treated to a meal at a saloon in my whole life. Up to this point, Mr. Heins had done the majority of the talking, but now that we were sitting down face-to-face, I began to feel a little uncomfortable. Was I going to be required to talk? I had not made normal conversation with anyone but the widow's children for many years. Even then, I tried my best to conserve words.

"Are you excited about moving to your Aunt Ruth's?" Mr. Heins asked. He was looking at me so directly and kindly, and this reminded me of my papa.

My child.

"I'm not so sure, sir," I answered while looking down at my hands.

"Well, she must be an enterprising woman to open an establishment in that part of the country. Do you know how she came about it?"

"I haven't heard anything, sir."

He must have sensed my discomfort and then decided to take up his stories again. I was so relieved. I was near tears with exhaustion anyway.

"I did have business in Winnemucca, Nevada at one time, and that's not too far from where you're going. I had to go all that way to buy some replacement heifers. I was just a young man still. Those were the good old days of cattle ranching. Your papa would have agreed. Can you imagine driving hundreds of cattle over such a large distance? Well, we did, and I have never had such good adventures. There was a man that used to frequent Winnemucca while he built a name for himself in the cattle industry. His name was Peter French, and his business ventures made him famous from California well into Oregon and Nevada. Well, Mr. French was in Winnemucca at the same time I was. We were at the stockyard, and that's where I met him. What a bundle of energy that man was! So much intelligence and spunk bound up in one slight man! When I shook hands with him, I felt that he could reach right into my mind with his direct gaze."

My tired, young mind turned that confusing phrase over and over...

Reach right into my mind with his direct gaze . . .

Years later, I would understand when I met a rare individual who could do exactly that.

Chapter 5
Set Me Down
1910

Henry also had light eyes and a directness that could read my soul. I could hardly wait another minute to see him as I went through the motions of dusting the faded furniture in that hotel in Denio. Aunt Ruth and I had already gotten cleaned up as best we could and then were keeping busy as we waited for the right time.

"Don't get dust on your dress!"

I hadn't been groomed that much since my mama had prepared to send me off to Mrs. Rawlings's. I did not have a twinge of dread on this day, however. I worked on keeping my head high as we walked down the street to the spot where Henry was taking photographs. As we got close, I could hear his joyful exclamations as he worked with the subjects of his art.

"Thankfully, Mr. Wright, you won't have to sit quite as long with this new equipment. Your family will have to keep still just a few minutes, and I will take several photographs to make sure we'll have the one you're looking for. Young Billy there, would you squeeze a little closer to your sweet sister? That's good now. Okay, hold it."

I saw Henry bend his tall frame under a black blanket of some sort to work his equipment. By the time he came out to dismiss the Wright family, we were standing just off to the side.

"Thank you, Mr. and Mrs. Wright. It's been a pleasure to work with you today. I'll safely deliver your photographs to you as soon as I can develop them. I think you'll be pleased. It sure is a beautiful morning, and we've been given the perfect light." Henry shook their hands before looking up to where I stood with Aunt Ruth.

"There you are! I've been waiting for you," He walked over and took Aunt Ruth's hand before taking mine.

"Corrie, you look just as pretty as I'd imagined you'd look."

He smiled at me, putting peace in my heart. There *is* good in this world after all, and at that moment, I knew *he* was it. The parched land that had been my heart began to sprout life. I was like the desert primrose making an appearance after spring rains. I struggled with what to say to this man. I still had not said a single thing to him. Not that I was known for talking to anyone. I had gotten by with saying as little as possible to Aunt Ruth, and she had never complained. I tried out my refreshed lungs and took a deep breath. I exhaled, and words raced out.

"When are you taking me away from here, Henry?"

* * *

This does sound like a fairy tale, doesn't it? Quite unrealistic? Yes, it was not proper to get married so quickly in 1910—people would disapprove. You have to remember, though, granddaughter, that there were no "people" to be concerned about me. I was an orphan, living in what was considered a forsaken part of the world. There was nobody back home inquiring after my welfare, and Aunt Ruth was planning to replace me anyhow. In that sense, she was helping arrange this union. Henry was just making it all so easy. Any reservations or doubts Aunt Ruth had were strongly dispelled by his purity...good cheer...that smile...

* * *

Henry took both my hands and gave a delighted whoop. Then he kissed my cheek, and I caught his scent—warm earth. You know, the clean smell of the earth on a calm day when the morning sun has done its work? Maybe you haven't smelled it. I have noticed that not many people take the time to observe their natural surroundings. Mrs. Rawlings and Aunt Ruth, alike, were always rushing about like hungry hens.

I had spent many silent hours with nature as my solace. In my oldest memories, I had enjoyed side-by-side silence with Papa in the morning air, the fresh smell of dewy grass waking us. Then there had been the cattle out Mrs. Rawlings's back gate.

My poor, dearest friends . . . could I have protected you?

Finally, in this desert home, I had become acquainted with the earth. It was in the desert that something had been reaching out to me in my silence with increasing frequency.

I'd been hearing whispers from the north ever since I'd been forced to move down to Mrs. Rawlings's. I'd always assumed it was my papa because it sounded like the sort of things he would say. I never took much time to analyze what I heard, but I was comforted by this connection to my old home. Then the moment came when I lost all hope and strength to go on . . . when I had forsaken Martin at the bridge. The phrases had kept coming, though, bouncing off my hardened heart. Boomeranging back from whence they came.

My papa had warned me about a hardened heart.

The whispers had found me at every turn, in California and now Nevada. In Nevada, there were no barriers to stop them. They found me easily, more frequently, across the open desert. Like now—

Everlasting joy shall be unto them.

I gazed at Henry before me, and I wondered at this feeling in my chest. Could he be my joy? Could he soften my heart?

I smiled at him then, and he embraced me briefly with such enthusiasm. In those days, it was not considered proper to show public affection.

Aunt Ruth interrupted by clearing her throat, "Corrie can pack her bag when we get back to the hotel. If you hurry with this photograph business, I can find the preacher for you."

"I will take the photographs now, and I have no doubt they'll be beautiful."

Henry was beaming as he strode over to his equipment. It took us twice as long to catch up with his lengthy strides. He sat us down on the chairs he had positioned there. Behind us were the few establishments in the town. There was Fred's Blacksmithing and old Madge's Livery Stable. I tried out my new voice again.

"Henry? Would it be all right for us to have the desert at our back, instead?"

"What a wonderful idea, Corrie. You two ladies will look captivating against that clearing."

To me, it wasn't a clearing. The openness beyond us was inhabited with countless specimens which had learned the art of survival. A handful of juniper trees posed with us along with their community of sagebrush and bunch grass. The gnarled, twisted trunks of the junipers told a melancholy story of endurance. Having provided food for countless natives, animals, and settlers, they had earned their place in our picture. The scattered remains of other trees indicated the usefulness of their wood. Their wood had fueled the blacksmith's fire, and many corrals in the area stood sturdy with their juniper posts and rails.

I had survived three years in this harsh environment with my loveless aunt, and it all deserved remembrance. Henry fussed over us, and I didn't mind. He moved our chairs, and the junipers could now be seen in the distance over our shoulders. Aunt Ruth was a stoic picture. She was wearing a black woolen dress and her tall black boots. A large feathered hat was perched atop her tightly-smoothed hair. Newfound emotions flooded me, and I surprised myself by reaching over and squeezing her hand. It looked like she was afraid to move from her pose, but her eye twitched as she stared straight ahead. Would I think of her after I had gone away with Henry?

"That dress is so beautiful on you, Corrie. It brings out the light in your hair and the blue of your eyes."

I enjoyed his earthy nearness as he adjusted my bonnet and gently tucked a few stray hairs behind my ears.

My linsey-woolsey dress was dark navy and would surely look black in the picture to match Aunt Ruth's. We would look like two women in mourning. What were we mourning, exactly? The fate of running a hotel in the remote desert? Maybe Aunt Ruth's spinsterhood? We had spent three years together without having a single meaningful conversation. I could be mourning the fact that my own family had banished me as a foreigner in strange lands. I would look back at these photographs and know the secret, though. My dress wasn't black, and in just a few short hours, it would also serve as my wedding dress. And Henry said I looked beautiful in it. I would no longer be an orphan. I would be *his*.

As Henry got ready to take his photographs, Aunt Ruth no doubt had her lips pursed and her eyes stern. At the last second, I couldn't help but grin—and then it happened. My shoulders started to shake, and a giggle burst forth. What a strange sensation! I was immediately five again, giggling with the twins. Despite my mama's warnings, they had toddled outside without a stitch of clothing on. They were so delighted to be in the open air and sunshine. Dandelion fluff was floating on the breeze, and they were attempting to follow it. What a beautiful sight they were in all their glory. Their giggles echoed in my ears. I giggled along with the echoes but also felt a tear slide down my cheek. A forewarning.

"Corrie?" Was that my mama reprimanding me? No, it was Aunt Ruth. "What are you carrying on for? I have never known you to behave like this."

I wiped the tear from my cheek and stared down at the wetness on the back of my glove. What was happening to me? So many feelings that I had stuffed away were now coming in a flood.

"It's okay, ma'am. I enjoy these spontaneous moments when I'm photographing. I captured several images—and one of them before the giggles, no doubt. I knew you had it in you all along, Corrie."

Henry looked at me with anticipation in his eyes. How had this man read my soul in such a short time?

"Would you two like me to escort you home to make preparations?"

"I think we can manage, Henry," Aunt Ruth replied as she clutched my arm.

It must have been that familiar clutching-of-my-arm that started to fill my heart with dread. I felt like I was walking into thick mud, and I could barely breathe. The memories flooded my head, and I began to swoon. First, it was my mama as she pushed me away from our home in Haynesville . . .

"This is a good thing for our family, Corrie. Papa needs to heal, and he doesn't need to be fretting over his favorite girl. It'll be one less mouth to feed. The widow Rawlings desperately needs your help, and you'll like being useful."

I was exhausted from weeping, and numb, as I caught one final glimpse of my childhood home and the twins, their thumbs stuck in their worried mouths. The baby.

And then, there *they* were, in my mind again—the bodies hanging over the sides of the wooden bridges, swaying in the breeze. Mrs. Rawlings was dragging me away, and I realized I hadn't lifted a finger to help him. *Martin*. He wasn't guilty of anything, was he? Coming forth as a son of the Indian Mary had been his only crime. She hadn't saved him, and neither had I. I was just like her, bringing trouble to everyone in my path, sharing more than just her name. *Stay clear of me!*

* * *

"Corrie, snap out of it!" Aunt Ruth was slapping my cheeks. I was lying, lost in my dark thoughts, on the dusty Denio street.

"Let me help her, please." It was Henry, squatting down beside me.

He picked up my head and shoulders and cradled me in his lap.

The lifter up of mine head.

Where had I heard that before? I looked up at Henry as he wiped my face with his handkerchief. It smelled like him. His eyes looked directly into mine. My papa used to do that. Such truth in his eyes! I had no doubt he loved me.

"What happened back there, Corrie? You were walking away with your aunt, and then you collapsed."

"Such thick mud . . . I don't deserve you, Henry. I left them behind, and I would surely do it again. My papa and Martin. They needed me, but I didn't help them."

"Shhhh, Corrie. That was so long ago, and you were just a young girl."

They know not what they do.

How did Henry know? Did he know everything?

Why these strange thoughts, and why now? I tried to calm myself in his gaze.

It was then that he kissed my forehead. Just a pure, brief kiss. How could something so small contain all that love? It wiped away all the darkness and restored me. I breathed in the scent of earth—*of him.*

Purge me with hyssop, and I shall be clean.

I didn't want to move, but now the strength was there. Aunt Ruth tugged at me so I would stand up.

"I think that should wait for the preacher. Do you have your senses again, child?"

They helped me to my feet, but my hand did not want to leave Henry's.

"We'll just have to be apart for a little while," Henry tried to reassure me.

A little while, and ye shall see me.

Was it my papa who had said this to me before? We would just be apart for a little while, but then we would be together again. But it wasn't true! I never saw Papa again. I had a moment of clarity.

"No, Henry! I won't be seeing you again!"

My legs felt like lead as she pulled me away from him. I looked back at him, and he just smiled and lifted his hand. He had perfect serenity on his face. *Shining like the sun.* I must be going crazy, I thought. I set my face toward the hotel and tried to shake the sense of foreboding.

At the hotel, Aunt Ruth went into high gear and was nearly tearing up the place. I was still in slow mode and very weak. She handed me an old satchel and said I could keep it for my belongings. I just held it there, motionless. I knew there was no reason to pack.

"You might feel like I'm anxious to be getting rid of you, and I don't blame you for thinking that. You're probably feeling out-of-sorts after that episode back there. I have always talked about needing a boy around here to do a bigger share of the work. Now I'm starting to get cold feet. The truth is I am going to miss you, Corrie."

She looked a little awkward standing there in all her black severity. She may have wanted to give me a hug but didn't know how to proceed.

"You have given me a home, Aunt Ruth, and I am obliged to you."

I could barely get the words out, and it felt like a fog had enveloped me. Aunt Ruth opened her hand to give me something.

"Please take this brooch, Corrie. It was your father's mother's, my mother's."

She handed me an exquisite brooch, and I was surprised by the weight in my hand. It was a cameo of a girl. I opened the face, revealing a lock of hair.

"I think it was worn as a mourning brooch. Pretty, isn't it?" Aunt Ruth was hoping I was pleased with it.

Mourning.

"It's truly beautiful, Aunt Ruth. I've never received such a special gift . . . I'd like to hear more about my papa and your mama."

This feeling of breathlessness was becoming a common occurrence in my young life. Maybe I'd endured more than a body could handle. I felt hot, and my eyelids were heavy.

"I'm sorry, Aunt Ruth, but I just don't feel right."

My words felt thick and were coming in slurs. I needed to go lie down. I held the brooch in my hand and crumbled onto the settee in the parlor. I was surprised by the flood of tears on my face because there was no sobbing or wailing. I hadn't allowed tears . . . since Martin . . .

"Corrie? Henry will be here anytime, and I need to go find the preacher. Maybe I should get you the smelling salts?"

"He won't be coming, Aunt Ruth," I said plainly. "We'll never see Henry again."

The room went black.

Chapter 6
Midst of the Valley
1907

Mr. Heins and I were back on our horses after staying the night at the wayside establishment in Canby. I had been quite sore and tired the night before, not having had that much outdoor adventure in my whole life. It was a little difficult to get back on the horse, but I was thankful for the sidesaddle. I couldn't imagine how sore I would be if I had to sit astride. The spring morning was cold, and the mountain range far ahead of us was topped with snow. I had never seen such mountains, and their beauty captivated me. Speaking of saddles, some of the mountains even took on a distinct saddle shape.

"As I was telling you last night, Corrie, Peter French took this same route with his cattle. They say there were over a thousand of them. It must've been a sight to behold. I never finished telling you the whole story last night because you were nearly asleep in your supper. Peter French ended up building a cattle empire up in Harney County, Oregon. He kept acquiring more and more land, and some neighbors were not too fond of him. Right after I met him, he went home, and a neighbor shot him in the back of the head. It was hard to believe that the life in a man like that could be snuffed out so quickly. He was mourned by many and was buried down in Red Bluff, where he had his humble beginnings. He might've been better off sticking to a simpler life, but who am I to say? I have done my share of expansion."

I nodded my head toward Mr. Heins but didn't say anything. I wondered if my papa had known about Peter French. It was the kind of cowboy story my papa would have enjoyed. We rode in comfortable silence for quite a while. The horse I was riding, Sunny, was a fine one. He walked at a good clip, and I didn't have to keep nudging him on. I wonder if he was somehow related to Pal, Mrs. Heins's old horse that I spoke so highly of earlier. There was that image again, even though I had tried so hard to erase it.

* * *

It was early morning in late May in Lookout when I awoke to the shouts of men coming from the street. I saw Mrs. Rawlings light a lamp and wrap a shawl around her shoulders before peeking out the door. A gentleman, Mr. Hunt, stopped to talk with her. It took him a moment to catch his breath.

"It's awful, Mrs. Rawlings. They found Mrs. Heins's prize horse all cut up. Its ears and tail cut off and . . ." Mr. Hunt let out a small sob. He struggled to regain his composure. "I shouldn't tell you all this . . . I'm sorry. We can't prove it—but we can all guess who did it."

Mrs. Rawlings looked pale in the lamplight, and she held a handkerchief over her mouth. My body had grown cold with the gruesome details, and I would regret that I spoke up then.

I set before you the way of life, and the way of death.

"I saw them yesterday, Mr. Hunt. Frank and Jim Hall walked over to Pal when he was tied up at Miss Esther's. They were whispering and laughing, and then they pulled his tail."

I retreated from the light as I spoke, my body shivering with fear.

"Thank you, Corrie, you've confirmed our suspicions. We are sure now that the Hall Gang and that Yantis drifter have been terrorizing our people and animals. We are hoping the Law will finally step in and take care of the trash."

I haven't yet told you some of the other deplorable events that had been going on in our area for that past year or longer. Do you remember how I said that Mrs. Rawlings's cattle were lucky to hightail it out of these parts with my papa long ago? Frank and Jim had been mutilating cattle, similar to the way they mutilated poor Pal. I had seen some of the cattle with tails missing, hamstrings cut, and deep gashes in their sides. Holes were poked in them with pitchforks, and even their eyes had been gouged out. Oh, the evil was unbearable, and I can't even repeat all that they did! It was a mournful thing to be out and about at first light and to see a cow in painful isolation, while the rest of the herd bawled at her from a distance. Once again, we would hear the report of a rifle as the poor animal was given its peace. I just couldn't let myself imagine Pal that way! I know that, more than once, the Hall boys walked around with a limp, practically giving themselves away. I imagine some of the cattle acted bravely in trying to protect each other. The head of an angry cow is a formidable weapon.

Then, there had been the schoolhouse. That sweet, little old schoolhouse doubled as a church and had been such a haven to all of us kids. Our teacher, Jacob Harden, was a good one. Kind but stern, Mr. Harden had captured our young minds with stories of war, heroism, and, of course, the occasional tarnished character. No one loved these stories more than Martin. He would sit back at his desk with his long legs stretched out and his hands behind his head. His eyes would smile in fascination and awe. He was a handsome picture. I held him in such admiration, unlike anything I had felt for my own older brothers. Martin had thick dark hair, and his eyes and skin were light brown. If anyone in our class was bullied, Martin would be the one to bring peace to the situation. He would step in with fists only when there was no other way. He and Mr. Harden were the best of friends. Mr. Harden was always giving him extra books to read or poring over maps with him. Could there be any doubt that Martin would never intend harm on the school or another creature?

We were all making our way to school one brisk winter morning and saw fires smoldering outside. It was our benches and desks. It looked like they had been tossed out through the windows. Glass was scattered all around. Books were torn and strewn everywhere—the ones that remained, anyhow. Others had, no doubt, been used to further fuel the fires. We found Mr. Harden in a state of shock, staring at the blackboard dangling loosely from the wall. He did not want us to see his tears, or his fear. Some unintelligible words were scribbled on it. Later, we would learn that Frank and Jim never, in fact, had learned to read or write. Of course they would be jealous of their half-brother Martin, handsome and smart.

He had a father who loved him.

Soon, Frank and Jim would threaten him and force him to go along on their violent sprees.

Now, Calvin Hall ended up being a lily-livered man, a straight-up coot. It wasn't love that drove him to aid the enemy living under his own roof. He was just too scared to put a stop to it. As Frank and Jim grew up, they had taken control of Mr. Hall, who was, as I had explained, Frank's stepfather but Jim's real father. It had started with name calling, jokes, and an occasional shove. Then they grew quickly in stature and girth and soon towered over him with threats and demands. From what I heard, they learned all of this from their mother, Mary. She had no respect for Calvin, either.

She no doubt reminded him, "You just married me for the sawmill and so I'd give you sons to do all of your work!"

The drifter, Daniel Yantis, blew into town just in time to rescue Mary from her weak husband. They think Yantis may have come over from Yreka after the townspeople drove him out. He carried a big rifle at all times and was threatening by nature. Mary Joe was swept off her feet, once again, and the two of them took up residence at a nearby ranch. Frank and Jim idolized him, of course, and soon their dastardly acts were more frequent. To convince you further of the weakness of Calvin Hall, I will tell you that he even harbored the man Yantis from time to time. He was the pawn of Frank and Jim, and now, of their new "papa," Yantis. They would vandalize the county and come back to the Hall place for an alibi. Calvin Hall never went along on their escapades, save maybe the stealing of a pitchfork. His crime was in protecting the evil ones and taking bribes of stolen meat. He was, in fact, in his seventies by this time and certainly would not have had the strength to participate in the wickedness.

As the crimes were coming to light, Martin was showing signs of strain. He was pale and thinner. I think he was terrified of Daniel Yantis. Yantis and his own brothers must have done something to scare him into submission. His once robust frame had grown slight, and his eyes showed fear and nervousness. It became rare for him to take the time to talk, and he avoided Mr. Harden. The sweet moment I shared with him, by Pal, was just a brief parting of the dark clouds that had gathered.

There was no Law in Lookout. I don't think you could count the nervous constable, Erv Carpenter, as the Law. Neither was there an official jail. The closest Law was a hard ride to Alturas. Mr. Eades and other men had gone there to make a plea for help, but nobody had paid them any genuine heed. Even the vandalism of the schoolhouse was dismissed as a misdemeanor. What about the cattle? It is common sense that harm to livestock is a serious offense. As it seemed that no Law was going to come to their aid, Mr. Eades rode with a posse out to Yantis and Mary's place and threw a strap around Martin's neck. He was badly shaken and told them that he knew of stolen items under Hall's bed. The men were unjustifiably rough with Martin and would have to find a way to keep him quiet.

They found what they were looking for at the Hall place and pursued Frank, who was riding a fast, green horse. Frank was able to escape into a gorge, but they caught him and threw a hackamore around his neck. They practically killed him by dragging him to the Gilbert Ranch, and they decided to end it all right there. Mr. Eades was set on killing Frank, who *surely* had stolen his barbed wire. (The truth about Mr. Eades, or Isom Eades, is that he was a "squaw man." Before his current marriage to an Indian, he had wanted to marry one of the Hall girls. Calvin, with a surprising show of backbone, put a stop to that. Eades carried a grudge toward the Halls, especially when Frank tried to run off with his wife. As you see, there was a bit more to it than *barbed wire*.)

Eades and the others strung Frank up over the rafters of the Gilbert barn. The hackamore broke, so while Frank lay half choked, they fixed it and tied it up again. It must not have been Frank's appointed day, for the rope gave way again. Mr. Eades was filled with a murderous rage and slammed his six-gun into Frank's head. They left him there for dead, but somehow Frank survived.

With Frank still on the loose, and everyone mourning the loss of Pal, some of the men in the town were ready to be done with it all. They did larger searches of the Hall and Yantis place. Over a hundred items were found at the Yantis place, including tableware and the hooves of a calf left in the woodstove. But harming Pal was surely the final straw.

Chapter 7
Full of Bones
1907

The last I saw of Mr. Heins, he was riding back toward Lookout with my gentle mount Sunny ponying behind. He had secured passage for me with a man named Smithy, from Alturas to Denio Station, Nevada. This was not a task Mr. Heins had taken lightly, but Smithy came recommended by an old friend. Still, he had lost a whole night's sleep fretting and praying over whether this man Smithy was to be trusted. Funny, I don't believe my own mama or Mrs. Rawlings had missed a wink of sleep before banishing me to some alien place. I was thankful that Mr. Heins cared enough to pray, although I had never learned to pray myself. I had vague memories of my papa speaking as if to the air. It sounded like a one-sided conversation to me. Had he been praying?

He would say things like, "What would you have me do?" and "You sure gave us something extra special this time" and "I'll place my trust in you." Most often, it was, "Forgive my weakness and my wicked thoughts."

I bet he was speaking of my mama then. How could he not feel ill will toward a woman who defied him so frequently? She had nearly turned the whole family against him. Not me, though, or the twins. I made sure that the twins knew how kind and hardworking their papa was. I wanted them to know that there was nothing that man couldn't do. The twins would look up at me and just eat up my every word. He may as well have been King David in their eyes, killing both a lion and a bear with his bare hands. I had not learned to pray, however. It seemed my life was already set on a course not of my choosing, so what was the point in taking up a plea?

Mr. Heins did look weary that morning. He reached into his vest pocket and pulled out a folded handkerchief. He came over to where I was seated in the wagon and leaned over to whisper in my ear.

"Here's a little something for an emergency. Keep a distance between yourself and any strangers, and I think you'll be all right. I have peace, and I believe there are good things in your future, Corrie. Look for them."

The handkerchief was heavy with a coin, but I didn't look. He had also handed me a small pocketknife. It was also heavy for its size, but feminine in appearance, and had a mother of pearl handle. I wondered if his wife had sent it along for me. I quickly pushed them into the upper of my boot.

"Thank you, Mr. Heins, for everything."

"Everyone should always keep a knife handy," he whispered.

He took my hand and gave it a quick kiss. He had treated me like a lady. He got onto his horse and waited for Smithy to make his final preparations.

"Have you taken into account the cold spring nights?" Mr. Heins questioned Smithy.

"Most definitely, sir," Smithy assured him.

Mr. Heins's friend cleared his throat. "Smithy hasn't worked as a blacksmith, as you might've assumed. He's a supply man and makes these trips frequently. His odd habits are unappealing, to be sure, but his only true faults that I've caught wind of are his preference to Indians over whites and his diet. As far as I know, he eats only plain hard-boiled eggs—so he, consequently, smells like one. I hope you don't have to be downwind of him too often, Miss."

"Well," Mr. Heins had replied to his friend, "I guess a hard-boiled egg is harmless enough, and maybe he knows something about the Indians that we don't. Maybe the whites have done him wrong. Either way, my Corrie sounds like she'd be safer with him than others, as far as the Indians are concerned."

My Corrie, he had said. That is what Papa used to say. If my heart hadn't been long broken, I think it would have broken then.

I am His, and He is mine.

It was the line of a song that came to my ears just then. My papa used to sing it, and I heard the words in his voice. Why was I hearing him now? I fidgeted in my seat.

His forever, only His.

"Mr. Smithy, if you don't mind, we'd better get moving." My voice and its hardness surprised me. I must have been looking to avoid a dramatic goodbye, and the quicker we left, the better.

Smithy eyeballed me as he addressed Mr. Heins. "Yes, sir, there is a tolerable couple who takes in travelers near Nut Mountain. We will reach it in a few days, Lord willing, and Miss Corrie will have a reprieve there."

"That sounds just fine, thank you. Godspeed then." Mr. Heins tipped his hat to us and turned his horse.

I did not say goodbye, and it was cowardly. I did not trust myself to keep my composure. Mr. Heins was the only person living who had treated me so kindly, and now we were parting. I felt like a crumbling, earthen vessel that had just taken another blow. I was now being carried east to the potsherd's gate, most likely to be cast aside and remembered no more.

"Well, Miss Corrie," Smithy interrupted my melancholy musings, "did you know that Alturas is famous for a really big trial some years back? The grand jury indicted several members of a lynch mob from the Big Valley area. Of course, they would've kept it a secret from you, the whole grisly affair—you being so young and all. The state was outraged when the mob was not brought to justice locally. Things started happening when an anonymous letter named thirteen of the lynch mob. Soon, the town was teeming with reporters—even bounty hunters! There were at least twenty more men who could have been indicted, too. They tried one man, Brown, for the hanging of the young boy. I think his name was Martin—he was only thirteen! The lynch mob must've killed him to keep him quiet. Just like they silenced Calvin Hall—poor old soul! The costly trial was an outright mess. It lasted ninety days, and Brown was found not guilty. Just a few years later, Brown died in a train wreck. The whole thing was such a tragedy."

I did not respond. I was thinking on what this stranger had just said. He was wrong—nobody had shielded me. *I had seen the whole grisly affair . . . I was even to blame . . .* Could I have been brought to trial for inciting the men against the Hall Gang? But Martin's murderer had been found not guilty. Could I let go of the guilt?

Smithy continued, "After this journey, you'll truly feel like you have seen the elephant!"

I'm not quite sure I understood what he meant, but I know my mama had used that phrase before. I'm uncertain if it was having twelve kids that sent her over the edge or maybe it was the trip west, but she would often talk to herself.

"John was so set on seeing the elephant that he never took any account of my opinion. My folks would've set us up real nice with some farmland in Arkansas if that's what he really wanted. Then I would've had my mama's help with all these young'uns, and maybe we would've had a reason to clean up now and then. Oh no, but he needed to prove his manhood. There's no point in wearing anything fancy in this forsaken place. There's no frolicking here. It's just day-in-and-day-out drudgery. Some elephant!" With that, she would throw the nearest object against the wall. We all knew to keep clear whenever she went into one of these monologues.

So Smithy had piqued my curiosity with that statement about "seeing the elephant." *Curiosity* was a new adventure, but not quite *hope*, a feeling I had tucked away. I had no *fear*, just a feeling of resignation. All the troubles in my young life had been weaning me off the world, anyhow. I had nothing worth clinging to. I was just a tired vessel waiting to be discarded and crushed.

As soon as we left Alturas, Smithy rustled around in his pack for an egg. I saw he had a real knack for peeling them. He held the reins between his knees, gave the egg a few thumps on the buckboard, and with some quick flicking motions, he had it peeled. He popped it in his mouth and then turned to me and asked if I wanted one. Seeing his mouth full of egg settled my mind that I would not be wanting one. Well, that answered any questions there may have been about food rations. I had the food that Mr. Heins had provided, and Smithy had his sack of eggs.

We were traveling northeast from Alturas, and we soon crossed over a river. My bones told me it was the Pit River again. Would I ever be free of its mournful reminders and accusing whispers? It ran on our left for quite a distance, and then we finally made a right turn toward a mountain pass. This was the juncture where I could leave that cursed river behind.

As you may have already guessed, I was a very inward-focused adolescent. I suppose it's more correctly called "introverted." I would fall into these trancelike states, staring out into the horizon. In this manner, I did not always absorb everything being said around me. Only if something really sparked my interest would I hear it. Thankfully, this worked out well for Smithy and me. He talked as if he didn't care if I was listening or not. I imagine he talked this way even when he did not have a passenger. I surprised myself, however, and found I was listening quite often to his ramblings. Curious, I rather enjoyed his knowledge of the flora and fauna that surrounded us. Smithy's father had been a horseshoer, and they would often travel together through this country. In this way, he had gained an appreciation for the desert. Their friendship with the Indians had no doubt aided their education. Did you know that a horseshoer was really a "shoeing smith" for horses? Thus, Smithy's name.

"Oh, no, don't touch those, Miss Corrie!" Smithy drew me away from my thoughts. "That plant is the stinging nettle. Once you're used to it, it isn't so bad, but your young skin would not like it at all. It kind of puckers you up. It makes a very good tea, though. See, people think I only eat eggs, but I do take some medicinals now and then. I think I have the healthiest diet of any white man. I won't touch coffee. You shouldn't, either—it just sucks the life out of you. I'll boil you some stinging nettle tea, and you'll taste the nutrition firsthand!"

I actually liked coffee when Mrs. Rawlings would let me have a small cup during our early morning baking. I was willing to consider what Smithy said, however. I could tell that this trip would not be boring. We were crossing over what Smithy called Cedar Pass, headed into Surprise Valley which would be the end of California for me. Smithy had stopped and was collecting nettles and other plants from among the abundant greenery. He said that fresh greens would be harder to find once we got into Nevada. Despite his warning, I was tempted and decided I would touch the stinging nettles after all. Having lived such a numb existence for so long, I think that I wanted to feel something—anything. Even pain might bear witness to the fact that I was living. Besides, Smithy was grabbing them up by the handfuls with his *bare* hands.

"You only want to use the fresh spring leaves. They hold the most vitamins," Smithy said with a grin. He really got excited about anything *plants*.

The stinging nettles jutted out along the streambed in clusters. I went a little ways beyond Smithy. We were in a spot where the quaking aspen mingled with the pines. The wind was causing the aspen leaves to play a soothing, rustling melody. There was a smell like fresh cut onion all around, and my senses were on overload. I stood there and lost myself in the sounds of the creek, and the trees, and the smell of what must have been wild onion. Everything around me was vibrant with life and expectancy. Such a contrast to the void within.

According to Smithy, the stinging nettles and onions and countless species were growing for our benefit in the hopes that we would render them useful.

"How sad if they just grew here unnoticed and unharvested," he said in all sincerity.

About that time, I had ever so lightly let the tips of my fingers run over some of the swaying stinging nettles. I had prepared myself to not utter a sound, but a quiet "oh" escaped my lips as it felt like a thousand needles had found their way into my fingertips. Smithy was right, my skin felt like it was puckering. It was not a feeling of pain, but just a very odd, startling sensation.

"Uh, oh, Miss Corrie, did they get you? It happens! You can be walking around unawares, and they'll make themselves known. Good thing our Creator put a remedy right next to the nettles for that sting. Do you see those big leaves growing right out of the ground alongside the stinging nettles? Those are dock leaves. Take one, crush it a bit, and then wrap it around your fingertips. Make sure the veiny part is the side touching your skin. Isn't that convenient?"

The veiny part . . . the lifeblood . . .

Just as I had hoped, I felt more alive in that moment than I had for years. Smithy was chatting up a storm while making sure I was feeling better, that dock leaf held tightly to my fingers. I felt comforted and wondered if Smithy could find a remedy for everything that ailed me.

Chapter 8
Behold
1910

As the blackness opened up to the pale light of Aunt Ruth's parlor in Denio, I was thinking back to that day with Smithy on Cedar Pass, the dock leaf seeping its life out all over me—like a balm. It took the sting.

The sting of death is sin.

By whose stripes ye were healed.

Sin . . . stripes . . . whose stripes? I didn't understand. I was lying on Aunt Ruth's settee and thinking of those phrases that had come to me, as if on air. Tears were quietly but steadily flowing. With my awakened conscience, I was awakened to the knowledge that I would not be seeing Henry again.

He had been *life* to me in that brief time—my remedy. He had shown me the possibility of truly living, and now I knew he was gone. My soul felt the vacancy.

"Oh, I see you're awake now, Corrie. You were in a dead faint. How did you know that Henry left?" Aunt Ruth did not wait for my answer but kept on with her excited rendering of the events. "It's the strangest thing, but no one can find the slightest trace of him—save for our photographs. How did he manage to make our photographs and then vanish? I thought developing photographs took more time."

Henry had kept his word to the Wright family and delivered their photographs to them.

Later, they found the other photographs stacked neatly on a bench on the Wright's front porch.

"Well, I don't know where he made off to. I thought he was headed over to the hotel," Mr. Wright said, perplexed. "He sure was in a happy mood. He said something about an engagement and the happiest day of his life. We said goodbye and closed the door. My wife said she couldn't help but peek out the window at him. She commented on what a handsome, long-legged young fellow he was. 'I think he'll make it to the hotel in just three strides!' she had said."

"Mr. Wright looked a little flustered then, and he didn't want to say more," Aunt Ruth said. "I am truly flabbergasted and appalled at what has happened. I'd taken Henry to be an honorable young man. I never expected him to hightail it out of town."

"He didn't, Aunt Ruth. Don't you think he would've gotten his money first?"

It was hard to get my words out, but I never would give a moment's thought that Henry had done anything wrong. There was not a stitch of ill will in his character. In fact, now that I considered the two, he was a lot like Smithy . . . full of anticipation and *trust* in something bigger than himself. It was like both of them were marching in blissful obedience to some higher authority. Henry had somehow vanished—that was all. Just like every good person that had ever been in my life.

"That's true. Mr. Wright mentioned that he forgot to pay Henry and, in fact, hadn't had the opportunity. He said Henry was just itching to get back to the hotel. If he didn't sneak away, then what happened?"

I lay there while Aunt Ruth rustled about in her heavy, black wool, musing about the mystery. I may have forgotten to tell you before, but Aunt Ruth was a big woman, and that black wool dress must have been a seamstress's life work.

"I'm sorry, Corrie. You must be in pieces! Here, you thought it to be your wedding day, and now, it's more like a funeral. Maybe it's that brooch I gave to you. It's a mourning brooch, after all, and perhaps it brought a curse over everything. You can still keep it, though, dear, if you'd like. You're the closest relative I have, and it's rightly yours."

Dear

Aunt Ruth was suddenly showering me with such affection. What did she have planned? The heavy brooch was still in my hand, and I was content to keep it. My life had been a life of mourning, after all, and it was fitting. It was meant for me. Maybe my distant relative had also lived a pitiful existence.

"Well, do you want to see the photographs? I think they turned out real nice."

Aunt Ruth handed me the photographs and then left the parlor. There were three of them altogether. The first one showed our stoic poses, with chins held high as Henry had instructed. Although we were not smiling, I could detect a smile in my eyes. *A reflection of Henry in them*. Aunt Ruth looked proud in her heap of cloth. She should be. She had made a nice establishment for herself in northwestern Nevada. She could hang this one near the front desk to be admired by all who entered.

The other two, I would keep for myself, among my growing number of possessions. I knew I would still be leaving, very soon, in fact. Henry had inspired me to live, and he had left me with a spunk that wasn't there before. I was waiting to find out *where* life was taking me next. These photographs would fit nicely in my bag, reminders that I had once been on the cusp of great happiness. The joy within would have to sustain me for life, and I studied them closely.

The next photograph showed the breaking of a smile on my face. Henry was still written all over my face, and it shone. Aunt Ruth hadn't moved a muscle. Finally, everything broke loose in the last photograph. My eyes were closed, and my face enraptured. My mouth had freed the laughter kept prisoner deep inside. Aunt Ruth was looking at me with a puzzled expression. I laughed, even then, just looking at it. My tears were gone, and I would shed no more for Henry. He had done the work he was sent to do. He had shown me *life* and brought me *laughter*. That is when I noticed his signature down at the bottom of the photographs.

"Yours, Henry."

My two were signed while Aunt Ruth's picture was not. What a gift. *Thank you, Henry*. I took a deep breath and considered what may have happened to my benefactor.

* * *

It reminded me of a story Papa had told me from his childhood. I did not remember it until that very moment at Aunt Ruth's. Papa had grown up in Arkansas, near the banks of the Arkansas River. His own papa had run a fishing gig, and his mama had never recovered from his birth. She'd suffered a bad spell with her heart during his birth, and it left her bedridden. Papa's older sister, Aunt Ruth, had been the only other child to survive infancy. She was strong and independent, having had to take on the household duties at only age six when Papa was born.

Their mama was real bright and, despite her frailty, had taught my papa to read at a young age. She had just lavished him with every ounce of love she could muster there at her bedside. She had also taught him, as he had put it, "to lean on the everlasting arms of the Heavenly Father." I can just imagine Papa's sweet face looking up into his mama's as he absorbed her words.

She would plead, "John, I do know that the outside air is so important for your young body and mind. Promise me, though, that you'll keep a distance between yourself and that river."

"Yes, Mama. There's an old tree that sits back on that little knoll, and I like to take my book there. Papa found me a really good one about cowboys in the West. Maybe I'll read it to you sometime? If I go to the big tree, I think I can hear your voice there if you call for me."

"All right, John. Give me a kiss, and then I'll rest for a while."

My father was happy to kiss his sweet mama, and then he wandered out to find his tree. He could hear her humming one of her many favorite hymns.

"I think it was 'In the Garden' that day," Papa had told me, with a far off look in his eyes. He hummed and sang a line. "He speaks, and the sound of his voice is so sweet the birds hush their singing."

I relished in that tender moment of clear remembrance. I could hear my Papa's voice and remember his every word.

Papa had obeyed his mama and sat snug against the old sycamore trunk. He was soon immersed in the cowboys' misadventures and heroic comebacks. Papa fingered a worn rope as he read—he liked to pretend it was his lasso. It was in this frame of mind that his eyes beheld a disturbing sight that he could scarcely believe.

He saw a young bull, or maybe a heifer—he had learned those terms in his books—floating down the river, bawling, trying to keep its head afloat. This looked to be a desperate situation to little John. He did not feel so little at that moment, however, still puffed up with cowboy fantasy. He could hear his mama calling, and he imagined that she was a damsel in distress, begging him to please rescue her dear pet.

Would you believe that my young papa actually managed to get that flimsy old rope around the neck of the calf as it passed? He figured his muscles would easily be able to pull it from the river.

"I should have used the tree for leverage," Papa commented.

As it was, he had dug his heels into that river bottom soil, which did not help for even a second. He skidded behind that floating animal right into the powerful muddy waters of the Arkansas. The cold water immediately awakened him to the reality that he was just a little boy, not a cowboy, and he wanted his mama. He released the rope after the first onslaught of water into his face. He struggled and saw the head of the poor animal bobbing out of sight. Papa's struggle only lasted a minute as he did not know how to swim. He said it was so quiet under the water compared to the frantic noises above. I could imagine my papa looking around, wild eyed, into the muddy waters, and choking. I was not appreciating the story any longer. I still did not know how to swim. I covered my head with my arms and didn't want to listen.

"Then, he was there!" Papa exclaimed, smiling, lifting my head with his hand. "I bet it would have been the last time that I'd have surfaced the water, but that's when I saw him. A tall trouser-clad man, hat, boots and all, threw a rope and yelled for me to grab it."

"A cowboy?" I said in disbelief.

"I guess he was!" Papa laughed. "I just called him my rescuer. He yanked me up onto the shore and gave me a few good whacks to the back. 'Stay away from the river, son' he said in perfect tenor. You would've thought I would've been shivering with shock and cold, but I was warm. It felt like the sun had blanketed me in its warmth. The man said, 'Stay clear of those waters and fear the Lord your God.' I gazed up at him, with the sun's rays about his head, and nodded. You always obey a voice like that!"

"Did you get his name?" I was enjoying the story again. I bet my brothers and sisters did not know about this.

"Nope. That's the exciting part. I blinked, and he was gone. The sun was so bright, and I couldn't keep my eyes open. I think I even fell asleep for a while. When I came to my senses, I was still warm, but there was no denying I was wet. I could hear Mama calling, and I knew I would have to tell her the whole story. My rope was gone, of course, but I grabbed my book and trotted up the hill to the house.

"Did you see him, Mama? I tried to rescue a calf from the river, and I fell in. I'm sorry, Mama. But a big man pulled me out! You must've seen him? He had to walk right by your window."

His mama was weeping and laughing at the same time.

"No, John, I didn't see him. God must have sent you your angel to help you in your time of need."

Papa said his mama just held him tight and thanked God over and over for preserving her precious child. That's when young Papa looked over her shoulder, out the window, and saw the rescued calf standing on the riverbank.

"He cares for the animals, too, Corrie. My heart felt like it would burst with thankfulness."

Thankfulness

* * *

Do you see how my papa's story helped me figure out mine? I didn't have anything straight in my mind as far as what I believed about the Everlasting, but I had seen *goodness* itself in Henry. About the time Henry came around, whispers had been popping into my head with increasing frequency.

In Him, we live, and move, and have our being.

Henry may have come from the heavens to bring me back from dust, to repair this broken vessel. Now, he had returned to wherever he came from. In perfect obedience, of course. He did not leave me in despair, as you may suspect. I still felt the subdued beginnings of hope, and a longing to live. It was best to keep these thoughts to myself. I allowed Aunt Ruth the excitement of spending many a night spinning Henry into tales of desperadoes and malcontents. No doubt he would've been the sort of handsome outlaw that would live on in women's dreams, as men sought to hunt him down. Henry . . . hunted and handsome . . .

Martin

Martin, so goodhearted. He had been hunted, too.

Chapter 9
There Were Very Many
1901

The talk of Lookout and Big Valley was what to do about our resident outlaws. I heard more than one man whisper, "Let's gang 'em." Colonel Thompson, a local historian and commentator, had recently published an article about the trouble that was brewing in Lookout and about our grievances. He predicted that unless legal action was taken to halt the activities of the Hall Gang, "juniper trees would bear fruit."

I would never look at a juniper the same again, imagining the men hanging from their poking limbs. Many thought the western junipers were a trash tree to begin with, ruining the grasslands. Growing unheeded, they hogged all the water for themselves, leaving the ground around them barren, and inviting weeds. Those trees needed to be burned, and the grass would return with a flourish. Sure, harvest some, first, for fence posts. Juniper fence posts were the only ones that wouldn't rot, perhaps their only redeeming quality. But if the junipers had already ruined the pasture, then fence posts would be useless. Cattle would be penned up only to starve. Often called "good-for-nothing," the area's vigilantes would be forever in debt if one or more of the trees would bear the weight of the transgressors.

Like the junipers, the Halls and Yantis had few, if any, useful qualities. Cut them down before they could spread their vileness. They were doing considerable more harm than good to the community. Not only had they done the unspeakable by mutilating precious livestock, but they had rustled cattle and had vandalized and stolen property. I suppose stealing a pitchfork had been the pettiest of their crimes. Ranchers had seen their own brands on the hides of cattle found at Calvin Hall's farm. In regard to those innocent animals, a well-known proverb among the ranchers made it clear what those men were made of: "A righteous man regardeth the life of his beast, but the tender mercies of the wicked are cruel."

Anything good about those men was, in fact, not good at all.

I had been struck dumb with fear ever since ratting on Frank and Jim. Mrs. Rawlings could barely rouse me to do my share of the chores. The men would come to the house for pie and coffee, and to plan. I could see now that the men of the town were ready to take serious action against the evildoers. I heard the way they even talked about Martin. They were throwing him into the ranks with the rest, simply because they were all *hers*.

Mary's.

I had been so quick to defend Mrs. Heins's horse—how come I could not speak up now to defend my goodhearted friend?

The men were at first confident when they heard that the grand jury was in session in Alturas. Eades and Leventon went to Alturas to seek justice. Would you believe that when they arrived, the grand jury had already adjourned for the day? Next, they had hoped to secure the district attorney, Bonner, to come to Lookout, but he had a prior commitment in Lake City. Finally, a fatal error was made when a young Adin attorney, Mr. Auble, decided that the men should be prosecuted for petty larceny instead of burglary. This decision incited the citizens of the region, and they decided to rely on no one but themselves.

Colonel Thompson had recently commented, "When the law fails to protect life and property, I have always observed that men find a way to protect them." Due process may have been Martin's chance at salvation—but it was not to be.

Calvin, Frank, Jim, Martin, and Yantis were finally brought, with force, into the barroom of the Myers's Hotel, now a makeshift jail. Calvin was an old man, and it was pathetic to see him being led into captivity. What an old fool. A farmer of vegetables! Maybe he would've thought differently toward his freeloaders if he had raised more livestock himself and then seen them come to harm. Then he would've understood the connection between man and beast. Why had he been such a pushover? Why let those evildoers run his life? He had even used his political authority to get charges against the boys dropped. Unbelievable! I had watched from the window of Mrs. Rawlings's front room, and it looked like every man in the county, half of them on horses, had come to secure the enemy. This added to the dramatic effect, and it looked like a scene out of one of my papa's old Westerns.

We will ride upon the swift—therefore shall they that pursue you be swift!

I enjoyed seeing Frank and Jim getting their just deserts, but there was nothing exciting about seeing Martin in that condition. Tears were streaming down my face, and my insides had turned to rock. Unlike the three ringleaders, who were kicking and uttering threats and curses, Martin did not utter a word. He held his head high. His handsome face was calm, and he walked willingly.

No guilt on him.

Brought as a lamb to the slaughter.

My mind echoed with, *No, no, no.* But did I say it aloud? No, remember? I was a coward. I could have told them about the times I had seen Martin come to the aid of the cattle out back. One time, he had found a calf stuck in the wire, and I watched as he firmly held the beast to protect it from further harm. He had talked soothingly to it as he unwound the wire, freeing it to return to its mother. Another time, he had shown up with a rifle in time to kill a coyote that had been mangling the young calves. The cows could have borne witness to the kindness of Martin. The mama cows had joined forces against the coyote, and they saw Martin come to their rescue. I was worse than a dumb animal, though, and I did not speak up in his defense. I saw Martin glance over to the window. Did he see me there, hiding behind the curtain? His eyes should have been filled with hate as he searched for mine, but I saw only gentleness and worry. But, of course, he couldn't have known all that was in store for him.

Mrs. Rawlings had worked herself into a frenzy by this time. Her business was booming as people came by her place as an excuse to peer over to the barroom from her window. They would order a pastry and coffee and speculate on the outcome. I could hear every word as I rushed to keep up with all the demand. I was either doing dishes, mixing pastry dough, or scrubbing floors. Mrs. Rawlings even had Sam and Mildred doing their part. I was glad her children would not be growing up lazy like my older brothers and sisters. Sam and Mildred had been fortunate when Mrs. Rawlings took them in. My papa used to say that hard work was good for the soul. Too bad my own mother had gone against him and shielded my brothers from their man's share. They could've used a good soul cleansing.

"Corrie, you and Mildred need to finish preparing that rhubarb pie. We have only one piece of apple left. Thankfully, we still have rhubarb coming out of our ears. It will be some months before we can get our hands on any fresh fruit."

Rhubarb grew well in high desert gardens. It was the first thing to pop up in spring, and Mrs. Rawlings's whole yard was bordered with clumps of it. We canned it whenever we had free time. When she was feeling cheerful, she would let Sam, Mildred, and me pick a stalk or two and dip them in cups of white sugar. If Martin was nearby, she would even let him partake. It was a tart treat but tasted divine after a long winter of no fresh food. To this day, the taste of rhubarb instantly brings Martin's smiling eyes to my mind as we peered at each other over the tops of our cups. Women would be wise to always cultivate a rhubarb patch. I don't think Martin's mother cultivated anything but trouble.

I couldn't believe my eyes when Mary came to Mrs. Rawlings's during the men's confinement. She had never been inside, to my knowledge. She only bought a cup of black coffee and then seated herself right by the window. Ladies don't ever drink black coffee. She stared over to the saloon in silence. Who was she pining over then? Was she thinking of Calvin, her weak, but long-suffering ex-husband? He had taken her off the hands of Captain Wagner all those years ago. Was she feeling thankful or only used? Perhaps she was worried about Frank. I imagine he was her pride and joy. Full-blooded Pit River Indian, proud and strong—as she saw him. Frank was getting the revenge for her that was long overdue. She was probably tired of the disgusted looks of the women in the town. It gave her pleasure to see their fear.

What about Yantis? Maybe he was the one occupying her thoughts. How could she help him escape? Yantis was probably the true love she had always been searching for. He was younger than Mary. It sounds shameful to even verbalize it, but Yantis was only a year older than her own son Frank. *Mary Joe* had grown tired of all the older men who had been before him. Yantis's youth and energy gave her hope that Lookout would one day be in her past. As soon as they inflicted enough damage, they would be moving on, and they could have years together as outlaws. Yes, he was another white man, but he sympathized with the Indians and was jealous of all those well-to-do white men. He also wanted to see fear in their eyes.

I don't imagine she gave a single thought to Jim or Martin. Poor half-blooded Jim. Jim was doing his best to keep rank with his brother Frank. He had committed almost as many crimes as Frank, but he seemed to be another one of Mary's forgotten children.

She had always resented Martin. Martin's father, Tommy Wilson, had been too good for her. Handsome Tommy regretted going on drunken binges in his youth. He had been working on Calvin Hall's farm. His friends had dared him to spend time with Mary Joe—she had been a pretty woman, after all. What a tangled web that was, although Tommy never regretted having his children. He showered Martin with the kind of affection Mary never understood. Tommy had eventually found a sweet little wife who accepted Martin and Agnes as her own. I'm not sure why Martin had still been dutiful toward Mary and his half-brothers. Poor, naive Martin. He had shown them loyalty they did not deserve. Mary, Frank, and Jim had used him as their gateway into the white man's world where he was accepted. Nope, I was sure Mary did not give Martin a mournful minute. He was useless in her plans now—she had Yantis.

Mrs. Rawlings, her children, and I all stood, silently peeking out at Mary from the kitchen. You could have heard a pin drop. How could so much trouble sprout from one woman? It would be many years before I could think back to Mary sitting alone there, and feel any compassion. Was she capable of regret? All those men in her life should have made a wide path around her. Did they not hear the whispers of warning? Tommy especially should have heard.

Let not thine heart decline to her ways, go not astray in her paths!

Mary was like a deep pit out of which it was difficult to surface.

For she hath cast down many wounded: yea, many strong men have been slain by her.

Captain Wagner was surely thankful to have miraculously escaped from her snare. There would be no noose fashioned for him. However, the five men across the street in the barroom were still held captive with no miracle waiting.

Chapter 10
Open Valley
1907

I had never felt so much freedom as I did with Smithy on that first day over the mountain, heading to Denio, leaving my bad memories in the dust. I was leaving behind servitude to Mrs. Rawlings and going even further from my own family who didn't want me. I told myself that without hope, I could also live without worry. I wasn't concerned about what may come my way. I had lost any control over my life years ago. The steady jolting of the wagon had a comforting feel. I was simply existing and taking in the scenery.

We had gotten a late start that first morning in Alturas and had to make camp on the downhill side of Cedar Pass. We found shelter in a small depression with aspens all around. It felt a little awkward to be in a camp with a strange man, but Smithy had a way of putting your mind at ease. The simple fact that he never stopped talking, or making noise of some kind, made me feel he had nothing to hide. There wasn't a sneaky bone in his body. He rustled and banged his way through the belongings, humming a tune all the while.

"Would you like me to set out your bedroll for you? I figured we'd start a fire in the middle here and maybe boil up some nettle tea before we settle down?"

"That's all right, thank you. I can manage," I mumbled. I laid my bedroll several yards too many from the proposed fire pit.

"Suit yourself," he said.

My attempt to blend in quietly with my surroundings was futile as I tried to eat the stale biscuits I had left over from Mrs. Rawlings. My physical connection with her was slowly diminishing with each passing day. I was hoping the memories would follow suit.

* * *

I was remembering Mrs. Rawlings those years ago during that first week I was brought to her. Mama couldn't leave Papa to take me to her, so she had sent me along with a couple of men who were headed south. Can you imagine sending your young daughter with strangers on an overland journey? That is how she hastily dispatched me toward Lookout. Thankfully, they didn't mistreat me in any way, but I was still scared dumb to be in the company of strangers. It was a few days' journey, and I slept in the wagon when we stopped at night. Thankfully, they basically ignored me and were glad to be rid of me once we reached Lookout. Lookout was at the height of its heyday then, with enough activity to maintain two feuding stores: E.S. Trowbridge's General Store and William D. Morris's General Merchandise Store. It also possessed the Leventon Brothers' Blacksmith Shop and the James R. Myers's Hotel.

We rolled down the main street of Lookout, and I had a heavy feeling of dread in my heart. I had just spent the whole journey imagining what a widow caring for two orphans must be like. She probably wouldn't be much different than my mama, I finally concluded. The widow's face was probably full of lines and pinched up in a perpetual state of discontent. Papa was the one who had shared all the smiles, and without him, or Mr. Rawlings for that matter, I imagined it would be a mirthless place. So I knew her when I saw her. We pulled up to a dull yellow house, and there was Mrs. Rawlings, holding a baby in her arms, her hair pointing in several directions. A small, miserable-looking boy was standing close to her side.

Mrs. Rawlings was still fairly new at parenting when I arrived. She had recently adopted the two children after their parents had died from some sort of fever. Sam was just over one, and Mildred was still an infant. Mrs. Rawlings was nervous about bringing in an older child like me, thinking I would be set in my ways, but she figured I could still be a big help to her. Somewhere, she had gotten the notion that she would have to teach me submission immediately or I would rebel against her. I climbed down from the wagon with my small bag, and I offered the boy a weak smile. I did my best to avoid Mrs. Rawlings's penetrating stare.

"Now that you're here, we will just call you plain *Corrie. Mary Cordelia* sounds too fancy to suit you. We don't have time for any frivolities. It's a tough world to live in without a man's provision, and our focus will be *survival*. I don't want to have to force my hand with you, but I will. I don't have any time to be wasting on young'uns and their troublemaking."

Mrs. Rawlings was spring-loaded and ready to pounce at the first infraction. It was the third morning I was there, and we had woken before dawn to start making bread and pie for the day. Sam and Mildred were still sleeping. Remember that I was only five years old and had just said goodbye to my dear papa? I had still been crying myself to sleep every night and was desperately tired. The widow had summoned me for labor, though, and the sooner I learned, the better. She threw an apron over my dress and roughly tied my hair up with a piece of twine. Her lack of tenderness was just like Mama. First, we made the bread dough without incident and set it to rise by the woodstove. Next, Mrs. Rawlings was going to teach me to make pastry for the pie, and we would make enough for four pies at once. I mixed the flour and the salt well enough. Next, I cut in the lard.

"Keep cutting, girl, until the lard is the size of peas. This will make the pastry nice and flaky. All right, that will do. Now, add this cold water gradually."

If she wanted me to add the water gradually, why would she trust me with a huge, awkward pitcher? I trickled it down the side, at first, and stirred it into the flour mixture. According to her, we wanted just enough water to make the flour stick together. Next thing I knew, the pitcher went off balance in my little hand and sent a flood into the bowl. In the same instant, Mrs. Rawlings slapped my face and sent me and the pitcher reeling.

"You've ruined it! A whole recipe of pastry wasted, and there's nothing that can be done to fix it!"

I heard the children waking with all the commotion. Mrs. Rawlings grabbed my arm and yanked me to the back closet.

"You'll stay in here for the whole day, without food, to make up for what you've done. You've not earned your keep for the day. Now I'll have to cook *and* tend to the children."

She slammed the door and left me in darkness. I could hear Sam whimpering and Mildred wailing. I was left alone with my thoughts of Papa and of my new home with this loveless woman.

* * *

As I sat on my bedroll across the fire from Smithy, I tried to push out the memory of that dark day in the closet. Mrs. Rawlings's old biscuit tasted stale, and I almost choked on it. I stuffed the biscuit back in my sack and brushed the crumbs off my lap. As evening settled in, my mood darkened with it. Smithy held up his cup to offer me some of his stinging nettle tea, but I just shook my head. He grew quiet after that, and I soon heard snoring. My ridiculous distance from the fire left me feeling cold and alone.

The aspens towering over me whispered to me with the wind. "Who is Mary Cordelia? Who is Mary Cordelia?" They were mocking me.

It was as if I didn't exist and no one cared what became of me. I imagined myself turning to mulch overnight and blending in with the layer of last year's leaves beneath me. Smithy would pack up with a whistle, forgetting me entirely. Aunt Ruth in Denio would probably forget to inquire after me. I shivered and burrowed down into my bedroll, trying to block out the teasing whispers. I must have fallen asleep because I woke to Smithy giving me a gentle nudge.

"Just checking to make sure you weren't frozen solid. You shouldn't have put yourself so far from the fire. Let's try to leave before the sun's rays get any warmer."

I looked above me and was greeted by the most beautiful sight. The morning light was filtering through the aspen's newborn leaves.

They were gently quivering this morning, with not enough wind to cause their whispering. I forgave them then. They couldn't have possibly meant to hurt me last night. They were too new and innocent. Any wickedness was coming from my own jaded soul.

Smithy was almost packed, so I tried to shake off the melancholy and quickly pack my belongings. I focused on the noises he made rather than on my own thoughts, and this brought me peace.

After descending Cedar Pass, the world opened up like I had never seen before. It wasn't a green, lush world, but that was all right with me. The smells of Smithy's herbs, the sound of rushing water, and the sting of the nettles had accosted my senses. I felt at home back among the more discreet, the Empty.

"Now, Corrie, don't let this barrenness deceive you! There is more out here than meets the eye. It's probably why they call it Surprise Valley. You will be surprised at the riches of this valley. There's a lot of history here, as well as diverse plant life."

He continued, "My father used to distract me during our long travels with stories of settlers and Indians. There was one particularly tragic story, maybe true, maybe not, about some settlers who came through not too far from here just before I was born. It may just be a tall tale, but you'll have to decide for yourself. There is a convergence of trails twenty or more miles northwest of here. Have you heard of the men named Applegate and Lassen?"

I shook my head, anxious for him to continue with his tale.

"Applegate and Lassen were early explorers in this area, and their trails were used by pioneers going to the Oregon Territory or down into the gold fields of California. The pass was known as Lassen's Pass, at first, but was changed due to the tragedy that was said to have occurred there. According to the tale, some emigrants had camped on the pass and were having a 'fandango,' or a dance. It was a Spanish tradition. The emigrants were celebrating the resources of this area after passing through the dry flats. Maybe they thought they'd reached the Sierras. Or maybe they were just dancing to stay warm." He grinned.

"Either way, it's said that the frolic ended tragically when they were attacked by Indians. Every one of them was killed—even women and children. They blame it on the Modoc Indians, but as I said, it may just be hearsay. Some call it Fandango Pass ever since, and most people avoid its steepness in favor of Cedar Pass."

"So why do you like Indians so much?" I asked abruptly. His story had sounded similar to the one Mr. Heins had told me about Bloody Point.

"That is a good question, girl. Listen carefully to what I am about to say. It's important to first understand that all people are sinners alike. We have all committed wrongs against the perfect and holy God. This is far more important than the fact that we have hurt each other. It seems to me, though, that I've met more Indians who are ready to admit their past wrongs. They're more readily humble before their Maker. I've met many a white man who struts around, proud and greedy, with no conscience. It's probably easy for me to have a clear picture of the situation. I'm just a sojourner. All I have is this wagon and no particular piece of land that I try to claim as my own. It's land and possessions that'll often cause a person to sin, trying to hold on too tightly to a particular place or item. I've also met many Indians with good hospitality. They'll give you everything they own to make you feel comfortable. Many have found the Good Way, and they demonstrate peacefulness in their soul. If the story is true, those Indians on Fandango Pass didn't have that peace. They acted out of fear or revenge. Whites have done the same, and maybe whites even made the story up to use against the Indians. The heart of each individual will be up for examination and will have to answer for its actions."

We rested for the night in Cedarville, a small town dotted with impressive houses and barns. Smithy was unsure of how it got the name Cedarville. We didn't see any cedars. Poplars, however, were a common tree to see around homesteads, as they were a fast-growing tree for a windbreak, or just to make a place feel settled. Smithy was a wealth of information, especially where nature was concerned.

"How did you learn all of this?" The morning air brought on a talkative spell.

"Well, it all came to me sort of natural-like," he said as he led the horses away from town. "The Good Book even says that for the farmer, 'his God doth instruct him to discretion, and doth teach him.' I don't have a farm, but I like to think that I'm a farmer of all the goodness God has placed here, and there, for our use."

Another thing that apparently came natural for Smithy was the way he talked about God. God seemed to be woven into Smithy's very being. I didn't mind when Smithy talked about Him. He spoke of Him with tenderness, awe, and respect. He reminded me of my papa and Mr. Heins. Mrs. Rawlings and my mother, in contrast, only seemed to speak of God in anger or in blame.

"God forgot me when we left Arkansas," my mother would often say. "He didn't have any regard for me, and I've no use for Him."

Mrs. Rawlings would just use His name in curses that I would rather not repeat.

It seemed that my papa's eyes were smiling at me then, as Smithy talked of God.

* * *

"Corrie, girl, did you know that 'the light of the eyes rejoiceth the heart?' You have light in your eyes that our loving Father has put there. You have to stay close to Him if you want that light to keep shining."

My papa's eyes were shining. Now that I think of it, my papa's eyes were always full of light, even at the end when there was sorrow mixed in. What did he mean about staying close to God? I had felt so empty and dead for so long, I can't imagine that I had any light left in me at all. Smithy brought my attention back around.

* * *

"See, this is called Mormon tea. Be careful with it. Some people call it squaw tea or desert tea. I have heard of people overusing it, kind of like a drug."

We had passed through dried lake beds, or dry sinks, as Smithy called them, and were gaining elevation into some tabletop buttes. I had been lost in my thoughts, but now I came to, as Smithy had stopped the wagon to show me a leafless, spindly-looking bush with yellow flowers.

"It can be helpful in a bind for fevers or coughs, though. Even for pain. I used it one time when my arthritis was particularly bothersome. I think I'll harvest some now, in case we have a need for it. Later in the season, the plant has little black seeds that can be ground up into a powder for bread."

Smithy cut a handful of the stems, bound them with string, and tied the bundle to the side of the wagon. He already had done the same with stinging nettles, dandelion and dock leaves, and some plants that were yet unknown to me. Whereas the fresh, crushed dock leaves had been the remedy for my nettle sting, dried dock could be made into a tea for a bitter or tonic, Smithy said.

"Bitters are good for getting things going inside after a long winter. They'll clean your blood and impart vitality!"

Smithy's jovial nature would make anything sound believable.

"I'd like to try some of the dock tea," I told him. Maybe my system needed something to move things along, to "impart vitality."

"Dock tea it'll be when we stop for the evening! There's a nice pass through these mountains, and I'm hoping to make it as far as Forty-Nine Creek today."

I was in no rush.

Chapter 11
They Were Very Dry
1910

Those had been good days with Smithy, three years ago, rolling along in the desert with plenty of time to take everything in. In contrast, events in Denio, in the absence of Henry, were in a forward motion that was unstoppable. As I suspected, Aunt Ruth had a backup plan for me. Oddly enough, I was just as anxious to get things moving and to take hold of whatever life had in store for me. Whereas, before, I had felt a helpless lack of control in my life, now it felt more like a peaceful *trust*. Henry had left me with a strange sense of calm . . . in spite of the mystery and disappointment of his leaving. Whatever was next for me must be simply a part of some greater plan.

"Do you remember hearing of the Harrison family over near Dry Canyon? Their son, James, has expressed interest in you for a while now. He is a dark-looking character, handsome and mysterious if you ask me. They're a decent, hardworking family. They have an extensive sheep and cattle operation—you could do a lot worse. It's not that I want to be rid of you. I just don't want to see you pass up what may be your only opportunity."

We were definitely back to earth after our excitement with Henry. The sighs and blushing had departed, and we were back to no-nonsense good judgment. Aunt Ruth had been here long enough to know that good things seldom blow through Denio. James may be the last wagon leaving for quite some time.

Don't misinterpret my resignation for excitement. I wasn't about to jump up and down over this prospect. That would've been entirely out of character. I didn't have romantic notions for this James fellow—Henry had left no room for that. I was being sought after like a prize heifer, although James couldn't possibly be in it for my looks. I certainly was not attractive or voluptuous, nor did I have childbearing hips. Maybe my trim figure had given James the impression that I was a good worker. The lines on my young face might have given me a wise appearance. Sorrow, if anything, had put those lines there—and I was, by nature, as lazy as they come. Not that the desert had been a friend to my complexion. Hard, dry winds blew every day—women aged early here. Too bad I hadn't honored Smithy by keeping up with my tonics as I should.

"Minerals impart youth!" Smithy had shared. The truth was, James must have simply known that one had to search hundreds of miles in this state to find a suitable marriage prospect. I was it. Oh well, it was my ticket out of here, and I was due for an adventure. I longed to explore the desert again.

"Get it over with then," I told Aunt Ruth.

It took a fortnight to alert James of his good fortune and for him to come collect. Aunt Ruth had a couple local young men already lined up to replace me at the hotel, and she was busy training them. I was easily able to blend in with the background, as Aunt Ruth was acting as if I was already gone. Maybe she was purposely giving me a vacation, and I was grateful. Years later, I would reflect on that time and wish I had relished in it. When does a rancher's wife ever get a vacation?

I had plenty of time to reflect on the situation and imagine what James would be like. It was so odd to be waiting for my husband to appear. Instead of asking Aunt Ruth for specific details, which would have meant holding a conversation, I just imagined what James might be like. I would try to conjure an image, though, and it would be Henry who came to mind. As usual, my imagination went wild in my solitude.

Dear Henry, there was nothing to mar him in my thoughts. He would be forever perfect. The relationship was pure, and there were no regrets. I began to think I should call off this deal with James and take a vow of chastity. Maybe I should cancel the short sale. I could be married to Henry *in my mind* and have no earthly husband. This wild train of thought reminded me of a book that a guest had left behind. Aunt Ruth kept a small library for her guests, and they were welcome to trade books or just enjoy them during their stay.

I would often sneak away with a book when Aunt Ruth was busy elsewhere. Truth be told, I was quite lazy. I would watch a guest leave a book and, at the first chance, snatch it and make off to my hiding place. I had discovered that I was much more comfortable living in the fantasy of books than in reality. My favorite hiding place was a small alcove off the parlor. The parlor was seldom used and was usually kept closed to stave off the perpetual desert dust. I would make myself small and perch upon a small settee in the alcove. The settee was mahogany, upholstered in a dark floral pattern, and I would think of it later with great affection. There was one circular throw pillow, and I could make myself comfortable with the addition of a coverlet that I kept hidden in a small cupboard. From that position, I could see out to the street without being seen. Aunt Ruth had a potted palm by the window, and it hid me from view, keeping my presence there a secret. I would read awhile, and then reflect as I looked out beyond the palm.

The book that time was about Greek mythology, and it was my first introduction to Greek gods and goddesses. I could almost hear Smithy warning me to stay away from such idolatrous reading. Artemis, the goddess in the book who most struck my fancy, gave me a lot to think about. I was thrilled to learn that sagebrush, my beloved plant, had gotten its Latin name from her, *Artemisia tridentata*.

Artemis, the daughter of Zeus and Leto, was a huntress and the goddess of chastity. Imagine the pressure of being the daughter of Zeus and also the twin sister of Apollo? Zeus was the king of the gods. Apollo appeared to be a god with countless attributes, and he was worshipped for his beauty. Did Apollo get all the good looks while Artemis was born plain-looking? Artemis' mother, Leto, gave birth to her and her brother on an island while being hunted by Hera, Zeus's wife. Hera had dispatched a python to put an end to Leto. What a desperate situation! The story explains that Artemis was born and then assisted her weak mother in the birth of her own twin, the beloved Apollo. Did her mother forget her young heroine then and discard her, directing all her attentions to her beautiful baby boy? As my mother had favored her boys? Or did Artemis have the choice to either go and compete for popularity with her brother, or stay and live a more obscure existence? She was destined for the latter, and so she spent her days at one with nature. Artemis desired to remain chaste and to be a hunter. She craved solitude. *This could be me!*

I could relate to Artemis. My own mother was preoccupied with concern for my sickly older sister and, of course, for her precious boys. She saw those boys as her potential heroes. Surely they would grow up and help her return to her dream life in the East. I had directed my attentions to Papa and my younger siblings, showering them with the affections they needed. Artemis had, likewise, been a defender of the weak and a nurturer. I believe my older brothers had been jealous of me. They saw the natural bond of love between Papa and me. My mother had long ago severed any natural bonds they could have had with Papa, and they did not know how to restore them.

Apparently, Apollo had some sort of weird jealousy toward his sister. Of course, those myths leave a lot of room for interpretation. Maybe it was because she was a gifted archer, in close competition with Apollo? Or perhaps it was Zeus' great love for his daughter? Zeus had granted Artemis a life of sport with her own group of cyclops for protection. Wouldn't that be something? A life of chastity allowed her the freedom from the complications that come with marriage. A deep friendship developed between Artemis and Orion, another great hunter, and this was the perfect opportunity for Apollo to seek revenge. Orion was beautiful and a well-loved god. The two had enjoyed a pure companionship of hunting in the remote wilds.

They would challenge each other to races and archery games. Their laughter could be heard from quite a distance.

If only Henry and I could have had the chance for such sport.

Apollo could take no more, and he sent a giant scorpion to kill Orion. Orion finally managed to escape the fight with the scorpion by swimming out into the sea. Apollo then told his sister a tale of another man attacking one of her beloved forest nymphs. He pointed far off to a man in the sea, and without taking a closer look, Artemis skillfully shot him with her bow. He was pierced, and he died before Artemis saw that the man in the sea was actually her closest friend, Orion. In a passionate act of grief, Artemis shot Orion into the sky to be forever memorialized beside his faithful hounds. I remembered Smithy showing me Orion in the eastern sky.

Artemis has been remembered as one who *shines in the darkness*. Although untamed and independent, she took many opportunities to help those in her path, even her own weak mother. I grew woozy at the thought of ever helping my mother. I stared out the parlor window and suddenly recalled what my papa had told me about a light illuminating the darkness, like Artemis. He said the darkness would flee from the light, and it was as if I could hear him there with me.

Yet a little while is the light with you. Walk while ye have the light, lest darkness come upon you: for he that walketh in darkness knoweth not whither he goeth.

I felt darkness closing in on me, even now. I curled into a ball and pulled the coverlet tightly around me. The closed-up room had grown so cold. Where was the light my papa was talking about? I can't see the way, and I don't know where I'm going. Henry was like my Orion, and he had returned to the sky, taking laughter and light with him. I had been brave, looking ahead to the adventure of marriage, but I suddenly felt lost and fearful. Aunt Ruth had called James a *dark* man. Was I to be yoked forever with a life of darkness? A yokefellow with sorrow? *Papa, please light my way.*

Chapter 12
Son of Man
1901

I felt the same cold and heavy darkness that terrible night in Lookout.

Mildred and I shared a bed in a little room off the kitchen. The spring nights were still chilly, and the kitchen stove imparted some heat. Mildred and I had cuddled up together, and I couldn't help the feeling of sisterly affection. Sometimes, I would dream that she was my own little sister, my bedfellow, left long ago in Haynesville.

It had been very difficult to get to sleep the night of May 30, 1901. Mildred and I had lain there, wide-eyed, as the men talked things over in the nearby dining room. They were downing the coffee and working themselves up into the fury that would be required to commit murder. I am guessing Mrs. Rawlings also brought out the whiskey for the occasion. She wanted to do her part in ridding the town of its thorns. Most people in town were not privy to the plan.

There was a trial set to happen in four days, but the men of Lookout knew nothing would come of it. They were ready to take the law into their own hands, and nooses had been fashioned from new ropes from Trowbridge's store. After their failed attempt at hanging Frank, they had spent a considerable amount of time practicing their knot-tying. The men were determined to dispatch those workers-of-iniquity into their eternity. In their minds, Frank, Jim, Calvin, Yantis, and Martin had sealed their fate with their countless crimes and threats. There had even been a recent threat to poison the water supply of the town.

They had, at first, released Calvin, seeing that he was a spineless individual and had most likely not taken part in any of the escapades. Calvin had refused to leave the hotel. What misplaced loyalty that man showed! Maybe Calvin knew he was guilty for helping those men escape punishment in continually offering them a safe haven. If he had been a true man and a caring father, he would have given Frank and Jim stout punishment long ago—while they were still young and impressionable. They would've escaped this fate with proper guidance.

Better a whipping than the end of a rope.

As it was, their wickedness had rolled on like a steam locomotive, gaining speed. Finally, the men of the town figured they would place on Calvin the stealing of the pitchfork. But think about dying and going down in history—for that deed! Thus, the old man was held captive with the rest and there would be no chance for him to identify members of the lynch mob later.

I had started to nod off when I became curious about the five men over at the Myers's Hotel. Were they sleeping unaware, or did sleep evade them as they considered their fate? *Did Martin know this was to be his last night?* I couldn't stand it any longer—I had to go see him. I needed to be brave for Martin. I had always wondered what my papa had meant when he said that the cowardly would have their place in the lake of fire. It did not sound good, and I determined to not be cowardly this night. I slid out of bed as not to wake the now sleeping Mildred, and I wrapped a blanket around my shoulders. I was thankful to see that it was a moonless night. I did not want to draw attention to myself with a light. I knew I could easily find my way in the dark.

Men had been posted as guards at both doors, so my plan was to sneak around to a window. I had to go around a few buildings and houses to approach the side of the hotel. As I neared it, I could hear the piano and singing. What an odd time for the Myers to be having a hymn-sing! I climbed up on a wood crate to peer into the window. It was too dark to see anything inside, but I had to take the risk. I had to warn Martin. I figured Calvin would be asleep, being as old as he was. Frank, Jim, and Yantis had long ago seared their consciences, so they would've easily dropped off to sleep. I knew Martin was the only deep thinker in the group, and he would've stayed awake to keep his mind alert and to reflect on the situation. Hopefully, the songs were distracting him from any fearful thoughts. I tapped lightly on the window for what seemed like an eternity. Finally, I saw a figure approach. It was Martin. I recognized a line of the song and saw Martin's mouth moving with the words.

"On Christ, the solid rock I stand, all other ground is sinking sand, all other ground is sinking sand."

He got really close to the thick-paned glass so we could see each other. Even though his eyes were sad, I could see he was thankful to see me. He gave me a small smile and touched the glass with his palm. I put my palm over his. I brought him half a loaf of Mrs. Rawlings's bread and gestured for him to open the window. He fiddled with it for a minute but then shook his head. It had been painted closed. I gestured for him to break it, but he shook his head again. I tried whispering to him, but he could not hear me. I was getting angry. Why wouldn't he take any action? I stomped my foot on the crate, and the sound startled me. I threw the bread at the window in a childish act. Tears were flowing down my face. I was gesturing to him in an effort to communicate. I finally put my hands around my neck to indicate that Martin was going to be hanged. He just looked at me with the same somber expression and slowly shook his head. Tears slid down *his* cheeks, as well.

Why was he so set on dying? Was he just lazy, giving up? I didn't understand. Maybe he had another plan of escape. Finally, he gestured for me to go. He gave a faint smile and leaned his head over onto his hands to indicate that I should go to bed. I wiped my face and nose and got as close as I could to the glass. We stared at each other for what seemed to be a very long time. His eyes were so beautiful and calm, and I momentarily lost myself in them. The darkness was heavy all around, and the future was dim, but there was no darkness in Martin. How could he be so peaceful? I felt like a trapped, wild animal. If Martin gave the signal, I would've clawed open the window with my bare hands. I did not like how I was feeling. I wanted the peace I saw in Martin—but had no idea where to find it.

And ye shall seek me, and find me, when ye shall search for me with all your heart.

I already found him! I thought to myself. *Martin is right here.*

I put both hands on the glass, and Martin put his over mine. I memorized his face.

"I love you, Martin," I whispered.

He smiled, but I'm not sure he understood me. He slowly turned away and retreated into the darkness of the room.

He wanted me to get back to the safety of the house, so I obeyed him. I shuffled slowly toward home, around a corner, and then glanced back into an upstairs window. By candlelight, I could make out the figure of Calvin standing with two others by the piano. He was awake after all. I felt compassion for him then, after years of thinking ill thoughts toward him. I wanted to scream. *Escape, Calvin! Take Martin with you.* Instead, I hastened away, like a frightened mouse. I should have knocked out the guards with a rock and broken into the saloon. All my actions were cowardly from then on, and I deserved the lake of fire.

I would later be ashamed at how quickly I fell asleep when I crawled back into bed next to Mildred. A true friend would have stayed up all night—to keep watch or at least try to pray. You don't realize how well you're sleeping until you are abruptly awakened. As it was, I must have only been asleep for a couple of hours when Mrs. Rawlings shook me awake. I had been dreaming of riding horses with Martin. Martin was on a black gelding, and I was, of course, on Pal. We were laughing as we set the horses to gallop.

"Corrie, make sure you keep up with me. I wouldn't want you to get lost!"

Martin's laughter grew faint as he galloped ahead toward the swimming hole. He was a beautiful sight. I felt so heavy and slow, like I was galloping through a bog. I was sinking. Pal would not speed up no matter how I coaxed him.

"Faster, Pal, please!" I didn't want to kick him, and I was starting to cry.

I heard Mrs. Rawlings whispering with impatience, "Corrie, I'm heading down to the bridges to watch the goings-on. You stay here with the children."

I scooted closer to warm Mildred and wanted to go back to my dream. I wanted Pal to get to a full gallop and catch up with Martin. I was drifting back to a cozy sleep but then sat up with a start when I realized what Mrs. Rawlings had said. *They are actually going to do it. They are going to take Martin.* I heard angry shouting and commotion outside.

Something compelled me to get up. I didn't want to wake Mildred, so I quickly dressed in the dark and escaped out the back door. It couldn't have been much past midnight. It was easy to discern which way to go, as people used torches from the spokes of wagon wheels to light the way. The spokes were also being used as clubs to control the accused. The sound of the clubs hitting flesh made me want to retreat in the darkness, but those torches kept beckoning me onward. Many others were emerging out of the darkness to join the mob.

Everyone was heading in the direction of the Pit River—and the bridges. It was actually a very short walk. A longer one, maybe, would've given me the chance to change my mind and turn back. As it was, it was so easy to get caught up in the movement of the crowd.

I looked ahead for Mrs. Rawlings so that I could avoid being caught. Where did all these people come from? It was hard to see anything, being as small as I was. Do you remember that I was only eight years old? There was no one there even close to my age.

All the men, captors and victims alike, had barley sacks over their faces, so it was hard to know who was who at first. I figured out which one was Frank—I could tell by his height and strength. One hand had come loose from its constraint, and he was violently thrashing about. He was kicking, punching, and trying to knock people around with his head. One of the captors kept cursing and clubbing him. Frank managed to kick one young captor in the abdomen. I later heard the captor succumbed to internal injuries not long after.

There must have been at least two dozen captors in the mob. I was scared. Why had I come out here? There was nothing I could do. I was floating along, being swept toward the bridges with the crowd. I wanted to be back with Mildred. The air was so damp and cold. In the rush to leave the house, I had not dressed warmly enough.

I felt small and helpless. No proper child belonged here. Loving parents protect children from such harsh realities. Children should enjoy the age of innocence. It had been a long time since I had felt my age, though. I had hardened so quickly, banished from my own family at five years old. I also felt older with all my responsibilities at Mrs. Rawlings's. So here I was, lost in a crowd of large, angry, cursing adults. I would probably be trampled underfoot this night — forgotten. I heard strange words again in that familiar voice, questioning.

Wherefore came I forth out of the womb to see labour and sorrow, that my days should be consumed with shame?

Yes, why *did* I come forth from the womb? Labor and sorrow, my kin. Very soon I would also be acquainted with shame.

Chapter 13
Can These Bones Live?
1907

On our desert journey, I talked with Smithy more than anyone in my life, save Papa. My time in Lookout had dried me up like an old cow bone, like the ones Smithy showed me lying forgotten in the Nevada desert. I had left California too depressed to talk and chock full of shame. Somehow, Smithy's easygoing, cheerful nature helped me put those things aside for the time being. Or perhaps his tonic was doing its job. According to him, my liver and circulatory system had been given a much-needed boost from the dock tea he had served up last night.

"Corrie, your skin is glowing! Your cheeks already have a bit of rose color to them. Back in Alturas, you looked sallow, like an old onion skin. A stiff wind would've carried you away forever. I think traveling suits you."

I blushed over such a nice compliment. He nearly said I was pretty. I had never been called *pretty* by anyone before, although my papa's eyes had hinted at adoration. I was a runt, being born after so many siblings, and then my sickly older sister getting all my mama's nursing. I was like a stick figure with straw for hair and light eyes too big for my head. Don't forget the long skinny feet at the ends of the stick legs! I had looked at the Indian girls with envy. Some of them had kind, deep, dark eyes and such glossy black hair. Especially Agnes, Martin's full sister. They had meat on their bones, and I had to keep myself from reaching out and pinching their cheeks. Their eyes were serene. Mrs. Rawlings had said that my eyes would scare even a puppy dog. She said they always had an intense, threatening look about them.

"You look like you're trying to decide between pouncing or fleeing. You don't set a person's mind to ease. Don't look at the customers. You'll scare them off!"

I would've changed, but I didn't know how. The things she said made me withdraw more than ever, rather than changing me for the better. Martin had liked me. Martin was compassionate and could see that I needed a friend. He would just look amused and say he was glad I was on his side and he might have to call on me for backup if he ever got into a fight. Some backup I was.

"Corrie, can you reach back and grab me an egg from my sack?" Smithy's voice startled me.

We had reached Forty-Nine Creek the night before and were now making our way toward Vya, a small settlement in Long Valley. Vya was another location on the Applegate-Lassen trail that Smithy had mentioned before. Smithy munched through two more eggs as he explained that Vya seemed to be a dying area. It had been a very welcome stop for settlers, but not many people passed through these days.

"This used to be a hamlet for cattle ranching. My father had business here shoeing horses, and I enjoyed visiting the area with him. I made a friend named Slim, who lived with his Pa, on a ranch here. He taught me how to kill jackrabbits, for food and fun, with a slingshot while I waited for my Pa. He was sure accurate! Young King David may have found a rival in Slim. It's not an easy thing to shoot a jackrabbit, as they dart to and fro in all this sage."

Smithy smiled and took in the scene around us. It was still morning, and our surroundings were surprisingly beautiful. I had never seen so much sagebrush before, and I was drawn to it. The sagebrush still glistened with the clinging morning dew. Every drop of moisture out here must be vital. Smithy stopped and told me to grab a stem and strip the leaves off with my fingers. He rubbed his hands together, crushing the leaves, and breathed in the released scent. I followed him through the sagebrush, the rough, immovable branches scratching my legs. I mimicked him, crushing the leaves and inhaling the scent. It was an intense, exhilarating smell. I couldn't get enough. When I breathed in the smell of the sagebrush, it made me forget all else.

"Look around you while you smell it, Corrie. You're going to make a memory with this smell. Every time you smell sagebrush from now on, you'll remember this spot and this moment."

I inhaled from my palms again and slowly rotated where I stood. We were far enough from Vya that we could no longer see the old post office or other buildings. We were guests in the vacancy of the desert, and the smell of sagebrush would always remind me of its hospitality.

Behind us, I saw sparkling white rocks jutting up from hillsides. They looked like ancient villages full of small dwellings. There was a solitary rock that stuck out and took the shape of a shark's mouth. Ahead, towering above all, was a cliff painted in brilliant color, aglow in the sun's revealing rays. I doubted that much had changed here in thousands of years. *I belong here*, I thought. The desert was granting me permission to just exist. Everything was perfectly still. There was no rushing about, no angry voices, no goodbyes. It was where survivors found their solace. Those acquainted with hardship could rest in fellowship with one another.

Smithy quietly interrupted my thoughts. "The sagebrush is a remarkable plant. Many call it ugly, but there's beauty in its willpower. A sagebrush can have a taproot fifteen feet long, so determined it is to live. In living, it helps support hundreds of desert species that wouldn't survive otherwise. It even protects its own. I have been told by Indians that the sagebrush is somehow able to communicate within its ranks. If an animal takes a bite of one bush, it can send a signal to others, who in turn alter their makeup. If an animal then takes a bite of a neighboring bush, it'll be punished with a bad taste in its mouth. The other plants actually heed the warning of the first and put up some system of defense. Can you believe it? Our Maker never ceases to amaze me."

I was hooked. This plant was my kin. I must be a survivor, too, simply because I had not despaired of living. My taproot ran deep. Now I needed to know why I had survived. What was my purpose? To warn others as the sagebrush did? Who was my enemy? Maybe it was my mother or Mrs. Rawlings, but I'm not sure that was even fair. They weren't exactly following me to this place. They had probably both long forgotten me. I was thankful when Smithy interrupted this spiraling introspection.

"There's so much history here, Corrie. The way some people tell it, that hill over yonder may as well have been painted with tears or blood. We are very near to a canyon called High Rock. Talk about painted rocks! You'll see all colors there—deeper red, black, yellow. The many emigrants we have been talking about came through High Rock Canyon, thousands of them. I can imagine their fascination at what they saw in that narrow passage. Some wrote their names on the walls as a remembrance."

Things were rarely pleasant on their journeys, however. One man was glad to be through the canyon, saying it was like being "shut up in dark defiles." He might have felt trapped, without a way of escape from the Indians who hid in the canyon. The Indians reportedly would shoot and steal some of the emigrants' cattle and horses. They would injure the animals so that the emigrants would leave them behind. This supplied the Indians with fresh meat."

I was wishing we could go over to this High Rock Canyon, but Smithy said it was far out of our way. We needed to head toward the northeast.

"Why don't you just close your eyes instead, Corrie, and I'll describe the canyon to you. There's a little illustration I like to make. You have seen all the volcanic rock around and the rim rock that runs along the top of the buttes? Doesn't it look like someone built a rock wall up there? This is how the canyon looks, but just more dramatic. Those hills give way to massive chunks of volcanic rock. The rocks become walls that form a narrow passageway, and I imagine it was very hard to pass through with a wagon, especially with water flowing through. So, Corrie, imagine, first, the hills painted yellow. I like to compare it to the streets of gold that are promised in Heaven. Heaven's a place that is unmarred—unlike our earth. Heaven's a place to dwell in perfection, as our loving God always intended. Then, there are the darkest of black rocks all around, on the walls and even around at our feet. Look down, and you'll see shiny black obsidian rocks. They are razor sharp when broken. The black is the sin of all mankind, going our own way rather than the way of God, our Father. He designed us to live in perfect, unbroken fellowship with Him, but instead, we selfishly want to do the things we want. To walk in darkness. Like the broken obsidian, our sins are piercing and destructive, often drawing blood. They drew the blood of God's perfect son, Jesus--who had come to bring us back into fellowship with the Father. It's hard to believe that He would still desire our fellowship after all the ugly things we've done. All people have done wrong, Corrie—white, Indian, and all the other races of people on the earth. We are all in need of God's forgiveness. Imagine, then, a layer of red rocks on the hills with a layer of white beneath. The blood of Jesus is the only way to wash us clean from all the wrongs we have committed. He was pierced by our transgressions, but He can wash us whiter than snow."

Without shedding of blood is no remission.

Smithy continued. "He's our rock, Corrie. Like the unmovable rock walls of that canyon. Torrents of water push through that narrow opening, pushing the sand and reshaping the earth. The rocks stand firm, though. When everything in life seems topsy-turvy, we can rely on the solid rock of our Lord. We all must decide what to do with that knowledge, what to do with the blood of Jesus. It's a very narrow opening, and many people will decide to go another way. They will look for any other way besides His narrow way. People would rather stay in a dark prison of their own making, in the 'dark defiles,' rather than go through His way. He has offered safe passage to all, but not all will accept it."

I was feeling very uncomfortable as I did not understand all that Smithy was saying. At the same time, though, I was repeatedly hearing words of my father's. He had told me that life and blood are sacred, and not to be left to the whims of mortals.

I kill, and I make alive.

I recalled the way Mrs. Rawlings so quickly moved on after the lynchings in Lookout. She acted as if it was an everyday occurrence and a perfect way to bring in customers. I was offered no counsel, no way to process my grief. The morning after the lynchings, I shoved my feelings into the bread dough. All neatly folded and put away. Smithy's words were beginning to make sense to me. Those were *lives* that morning on the bridges—and not just the makings of another gory story. Not one soul is overlooked by God, and Martin was most assuredly one of God's beloved. I needed more time, more understanding. I was thankful at the prospect of more days on the trail with Smithy.

"Do you have any questions, Corrie?"

"About the blood? No, but what happened right here?" I was not in a hurry to get too personal, and I had seen a large pile of rocks.

Mary's relatives must have been here and done something wrong, I thought.

"This world's under sin's curse, and we are all its descendants."

Could he read my thoughts?

"Massacre Creek runs directly through here, and then Massacre Lake is north. It's been told that forty men, women, and children were massacred there after being followed through the canyon by Indians. Some claim there's a mass grave near what is called Massacre Ranch. The interesting thing is that just as many say that this was another made-up story. Indians did kill, yes. They killed Captain Warner, up north, and we already passed through the mountain range named for him. Whites killed, too. Can either side claim to be more righteous? Of course not. The only way to be righteous before God is to believe in His Son whom He sent for us. The only history we can be sure of is the one written in God's Holy Word. The rest of history is often fabricated to suit the needs and whims of mere mortals."

Smithy fell into an uncharacteristic period of quiet. He ate some more eggs and drank a little water. I ate out of the jar of stewed apples from Mrs. Heins. They were delicious and made me wish I would have gotten to know her better.

We passed another carcass of a cow laid out in an opening in the sage. Smithy didn't see her as he was lost in thought, or maybe he was praying. The cow's ribs were bleached white by the desert sun. Was this a warning to me? Should I be praying, too? Had she wandered there to die, or had she met with an unfortunate accident? We would never know. The desert did not have time to offer up all its stories.

Chapter 14
O Lord God, Thou Knowest
1910

It was early morning, my last one at the hotel in Denio, when James, my soon-to-be-husband, arrived for me. He had waited a fortnight, as promised. I had just put away my most recent novel, unfinished. I could sense that my days of lazing about were over. Aunt Ruth kindly offered for me to take any of the novels I wished. I was going to take the Greek mythology book and a well-worn copy of *Jane Eyre*. Was it just my imagination, or did Aunt Ruth hold onto that one a little tighter?

"You keep this one, Aunt Ruth," I said, letting *Jane Eyre* slip from my fingers.

Had Aunt Ruth lost herself in the deep, passionate overtures of Mr. Rochester? Poor Aunt Ruth! Maybe she still had a romance in her future—I hope so. I had my glimpse of romance with Henry, and its brevity did not diminish its power. Whatever happened with James was just a matter of numbers—one man, one woman. I added the mythology book to my collection, which included the book of rhymes from Mrs. Rawlings and a Bible from Smithy. He would be disappointed to know that I only opened it once in Denio.

"Thank you, Aunt Ruth, for everything."

She hugged me then, and I was surprised by the lump in my throat. I believe that our twenty-four-hour escapade with Henry had drawn us closer. I had witnessed a very human Aunt Ruth who could lose herself in a moment of passion. It was a once in a lifetime experience that I could ponder during whatever monotony lay ahead.

The hotel door opened, bringing an onslaught of desert wind . . . and dust . . . and James . . .

"Do you have your things?"

These were the first and only words spoken to me before he said his wedding vows. Something about the way he said them made me grab my bag and make a beeline out the door toward his wagon.

"Wait!" Aunt Ruth interrupted, chasing after me, bringing her own dust storm with her skirts. "I believe it'd be more fitting for Corrie to walk with me to the church. We'll meet you there." She pulled me down from the wagon.

James nodded and turned his horse toward the church. I stole a longer glance at his retreating figure and considered what I had noticed thus far.

He was close to my height, slim but solid. He had dark hair and a dark mustache. He smelled so strongly of aftershave that I knew he had stopped at the barber just before coming to collect me. I recognized it as bay rum. Mrs. Rawlings had had a leftover bottle of it from her husband. I wondered if James had asked his mother to iron and starch his wedding clothes. He was wearing a long-sleeved denim shirt with pearled buttons buttoned all the way to his neck. He had on new blue trousers and polished black boots to match his black hat. His shirt was snugly tucked in with no belt. Not an ounce of fat, either. This man was meticulous, and it made me nervous. Henry had been blonde, long and gangly, nearly clumsy in comparison. Nothing was out of place with James. I escaped for a moment back to the hotel and Aunt Ruth's looking glass to see if I had any loose hairs. I noted with pleasure that I had a fresh look about my face. Vanity had won out, and I had been collecting plants and taking tonics since I learned of my impending marriage. This would've made Smithy beam with pleasure. I was too proud to have James be disappointed in his choice of a wife. I was wearing the same dress I had worn for the photographs. At least James and I would match in all our blue. I was carried away in a moment of fancy and had decided to wear the mourning brooch. It did look beautiful and was my only jewelry. Aunt Ruth had fashioned together a small bouquet of feverfew that grew in a pot on the back deck. They gave off a strong, pungent odor.

We made the short walk to the schoolhouse that doubled as a church, and nothing stopped us. Nor did anyone make an argument against our marriage. No bog caught my feet. No, James was not lovesick and did not have a lunatic wife hidden away somewhere like Mr. Rochester. Nor did he disappear into the sage like my dear Henry. James and I seemed destined for the endless ages, and my imagination went wild. We would be a pair of curl leaf mountain mahogany trunks slowly growing and twisting into a gnarled mass on the side of a windswept hill, our root system growing ever wider, grasping desperately for nutrients. Yes, maybe I would've been better off taking a vow of celibacy.

But it was finished. James was all business. He had said his vows, and I said mine. He looked at me with a grave expression, but not unkindly. His eyes were very light blue, almost gray, and that, with his muscular frame, made me curious if he was of Basque heritage like many of the sheep ranchers in these parts. His last name was Harrison, though, so maybe it was his mother who was Basque. He gave me the slightest brushing of lips on my cheek—I mostly felt whiskers. He then shook hands with the preacher, signed the marriage license, and kissed Aunt Ruth's cheek. I did the same, willing myself to not grab on frantically to her soft, plump frame. Then we were off. Mary Cordelia Loren married to James Parker Harrison, Denio, Nevada, 1910. I was now Corrie Harrison.

We headed south and east in silence for at least thirty minutes before James asked me to throw out the bouquet.

"I must be allergic," he said.

Without a word or a care, I tossed it to the side, not even looking back.

"Do you have any known ailments?" he asked.

It was as if he was checking a horse for soundness. Perhaps if I invented something incurable, he would hurry me back for an annulment.

"No."

"Good."

Aunt Ruth had told me that the Harrison Ranch was in the Dry Canyon area, and it wouldn't be a full day's travel. On the one hand, I was glad to not have to make a camp with James, but on the other, I was nervous to be arriving at his home so soon. Would I have to meet his family today? Would I have to fix the meal tonight? I wouldn't have minded hours of desert travel being lost in my thoughts. I had learned with Smithy that traveling helped me to think through things. I needed more time to process just exactly how I planned to handle this marriage business. I hoped he liked hotel food — filling, but lacking variety. I knew only a handful of recipes.

I hoped I would not repeat my mother's mistakes. So how does a woman act toward a husband? I had no clue. I had only seen my own folks. I wracked my brain to try to remember if I had seen any other examples. That is when I remembered an occurrence in Lookout.

* * *

Mrs. Heins had arrived at her sister Esther's house and had hitched Pal outside, as usual. I was watching from the tree out back of Mrs. Rawlings's, next to the pasture where my cattle companions grazed. Mrs. Heins looked as beautiful as ever. She was every bit a lady. She wore a violet traveling suit with tall, white, laced-up boots. I wondered how she managed to keep them so clean. Her blond hair was braided and pinned into a bun beneath her hat. It looked like there may have been fresh flowers arranged on it. She was in such contrast to my mama or Mrs. Rawlings. Those two looked like they dressed at a run and never gave more than two seconds to their hair. I longed to run over and gaze at Mrs. Heins more closely. I imagined she even smelled nice. I heard her murmuring softly to Pal, and she pulled out a treat for him from her purse.

When she entered the house, I scampered to a lilac bush that bridged the distance between Mrs. Rawlings's and Miss Esther's. I wanted to be the first to pet Pal that day. Then I heard an approaching horse, and there was Mr. Heins coming at a fast trot. I kept hidden, and he hitched his horse next to Pal. He had what looked to be a coverlet bundled under his arm and a parasol. He knocked at the door, and Miss Esther answered.

"Hello, Robert. Won't you come in?"

Mr. Heins gave her a kiss on her cheek. "Thank you, Esther. You are looking lovely this morning. I don't want to interrupt your visit, but I wanted to deliver these to Suzanne."

Mrs. Heins appeared with a radiant smile on her face for her husband. "Honey, of course you aren't interrupting us. What do you have for me?"

Her voice sounded melodious and full of adoration for her husband. I was enraptured.

"It feels like there might be rain in the air, my dear, and you left without your shawl and parasol. I wouldn't want you to catch a chill and be laid low again."

"You're so kind and thoughtful, Robert. I don't deserve you."

He pulled her to him and embraced her. They shared a kiss. She fit him perfectly. I blushed to be so near this show of affection. I remembered my own papa trying to show affection to my mama. She always pushed him away and told him she didn't have the time. Once he had even purchased a ready-made dress for her and was excited to surprise her. He had said that the green would match her eyes. She had tossed the package aside and told him there was nowhere to wear it in that one- horse-town. He had told her that he and the children would love to see her wear it. She had ignored him. My poor papa.

Mrs. Heins told her "darling" thank you again, and I could hear giggles as the door closed. Mr. Heins was blushing, and he looked pleased. He whistled as he checked Pal's rope and gave him a few firm pets. He mounted his horse and whistled on his way. I believed then that he was the most handsome man I'd seen, save for my papa. I sneaked over to Pal then, smothering him with more affection than I knew I had.

* * *

Would I be able to show affection to James as Mrs. Heins had to her husband? I gave him a quick glance and grew warm with unease. I wouldn't even know where to begin. He looked so serious and solid, and I knew nothing about him. He did not look cheerful and easygoing like Henry. What if he didn't like me? I was trying to summon the courage to say something. To attempt a connection to this man who was now my husband. I was terrified.

I looked out at the landscape around us. We had entered an area abundant with grass and with only a few sagebrush scattered sparsely throughout. I believe Smithy had called it cheatgrass, and it was a non-native species. It had been around Nevada only a couple of decades at most. Smithy had introduced me to many scientific ideas, and one of them was pollination. He explained that most of the desert plants, including cheatgrass, are wind pollinated. It's as if they are cheating—living a lonely, solitary existence, relying on the wind to do their duties for them. It really isn't very romantic.

Smithy had asked me what types of flowers I had seen in my life. There weren't too many I could recall, mostly the lilacs that grew in several yards in Lookout.

"Lilacs are a great example," Smithy said. "Aren't the blossoms beautiful? And you can smell them from such a distance! They attract bees and butterflies that carry the pollen to other blossoms and help them reproduce. It's a very intricate and intimate process. Plants that are wind pollinated don't have the need to be as attractive."

I could relate more to the cheatgrass, I suppose. As much as I wanted to be like Mrs. Heins, a lilac, breathtakingly irresistible, arrayed in all her purple, I was scared I would fail. I would feel much more comfortable living an unnoticed, solitary existence. *Risking the wind to do my job for me.* I had lost any courage I was beginning to muster as far as James was concerned.

"I'm curious as to why you chose to wear a mourning brooch on our wedding day?"

I stayed in numb silence and grew warmer.

"Did you inherit it?"

"It's all I have. How did you know it was a mourning brooch?" I managed to ask. I was curious how this man, my husband, knew jewelry.

"You could say that we are in the jewelry business because of our opal mines, although it's mostly a hobby. I have studied jewelry and the trends. They don't manufacture mourning jewelry like that any longer. That one you're wearing is unique, perhaps even scandalous back then. Usually they were made with darker materials, like jet, a fossilized coal, or with black glass. It is a nice piece, although when I saw you wearing it during our vows, I wondered if you were dreading our union."

James removed his hat and ruffled his hair a bit. I imagine he still had loose, itching hairs about from his recent haircut. Or was he perhaps feeling frustrated with me? Maybe I should reach over and brush off his neck? No, I would rather die than to be so bold. He put his hat back on a little crooked and then looked over at me with his serious, penetrating eyes. Too much more of that and I might faint dead away. I'll admit that he was quite handsome in a fearsome way.

Sort of like locking eyes with a badger. You know you should run, but he is so fun to look at.

Dreading our union?

I pondered his words. I was only seventeen. I didn't understand what a *union* meant. I thought back to *Jane Eyre*. It was the only book I had read that dealt with matters of the heart. You can't count Greek mythology as romance. Or the old woman who had lived in a shoe. Jane had loved Mr. Rochester and was devoted to him with her very heart strings. She longed to serve him and meet all his needs. Jane had nearly died from grief when she couldn't be with him. Then there had been her distant cousin St. John with whom she nearly entered a marriage of convenience. She had detested the idea, and yet, there I was, in a marriage of convenience to James. Maybe it was dread that I felt. Breathing was suddenly difficult, and I think my body was going into another one of its episodes. I was sweating and hoped James wouldn't notice.

We were entering a valley, which I assumed was Dry Valley, where the Harrisons were settled. I considered what I knew about opals from some of the men who came to stay at Aunt Ruth's. I saw the opals they found, and they were the most enchanting things I had ever seen. When held up to the sunlight, the colors put on a dazzling display. Tree limbs, pine cones, sea shells, and even animal bones had been turned into opals in a process involving water and silica and I'm not sure what else. I overheard them say that the opals were formed during some miraculous events in nature.

This made me think of Smithy. He had talked about miraculous findings in the desert and had pointed out the petrified remains of one large tree trunk during our journey. He said there were remains of giant redwood trees and all sorts of other types of foreign trees out here. They had been petrified, opalized, or fossilized.

"Trunks like these have been dug up, and there are no intact roots. Corrie, how do you imagine that these trees and even sea shells would be found in an inland desert?" Smithy had asked me.

I felt very warm, woozy, and strange. I couldn't catch my breath. I looked over at the somber James, probably contemplating the mistake he had made in me, but suddenly, it was Smithy looking at me with a huge grin. I heard him chattering away about the wonders around us.

Whither shall I go from thy spirit? Or whither shall I flee from thy presence?

I saw sparkles and colors, as if everything had turned into one big opal. I was falling, and then everything went black.

Chapter 15
Prophesy Upon These Bones
1901

I had dropped like a rock when I caught my first glimpse of Martin near the river that still, dark morning in Lookout. Like the rest, my kind friend had his head covered with a sack, and they were all gagged. He was not fighting his captor like Frank, Yantis, or Jim. He did not utter a sound. Martin was not ashamed. His head was held high—*no guilt on him.*

"Martin!" I screamed.

He turned his head toward my direction, and now he knew I was there. I could feel his chagrin. He would not want me there. He would want to shield me from what was to come.

"What are you doing here, Corrie?" Mrs. Rawlings yanked me up off the ground where I had fallen into a heap. "You should not be here."

She absentmindedly pulled me along with the crowd. It grew colder now that we were right next to the Pit River, and a mist rose off the water. The name of the river was so fitting to what it would soon witness.

Our teacher, Mr. Harden, had told us that the Pit River was named for the pits that the Achomawi Indians would dig to trap animals by the river. Who were the trapped now? Who had dug this *pit*?

Mary, of course. She had dug a deep, dark pit and watched as, one by one, all her men had tumbled in. I saw her then, almost hidden by a lone tree. There had been talk of hanging her, too, and maybe one of her daughters. Mary was an Achomawi Indian, renamed the Pit River Indians. She looked small and alone, but I had no compassion. I was filled with contempt for her.

She should do something! Lift even one finger to make it right again. Offer to take their place!

The sight of Frank, Jim, or Yantis did not invoke compassion, either. Where was Calvin? Maybe they'd decided to leave him alone.

Mr. Harden was there, too. I saw him approach Martin's captors and make a plea. He had been running and stumbling to keep up. Dear teacher. I couldn't hear what was being said over the shouts. I saw Mr. Harden reached out and give one of Martin's captors a shove, to get his attention. He and the other captors just kept moving. They were like a black storm cloud whose destruction could not be deterred. I hoped Martin heard Mr. Harden's attempt. I hoped he knew, then, that he was loved.

Frank was still putting up a big fight, and it took four men to secure him on the smaller bridge over the slough. Later, I learned that at formal hangings, there would be someone there to administer a prayer and to allow the condemned to speak. These men weren't given the opportunity. They weren't treated any better than animals at a slaughterhouse, where speed and efficiency were the goals. This was murder. Frank wasn't given a moment's pause, and I looked away from the struggle. I covered my face and ears with Mrs. Rawlings's apron, and she stiffly put her arm over me. I tried to imagine myself anywhere but there.

* * *

I was standing with my papa in Haynesville, near the area we used as a dump at the back of the property. Old lumber stood in a stack, alongside rolled-up, rusted wire and metal beams. A small shed stood at one corner, and Papa said the family had lived in that while he had first built their house. There were several barrels nearby where we burned our household trash. Far off to one side was the pit. The pit was where Papa would drag any of our animals that had died. Today it was the dog, Red, my brother's mongrel. Papa had just put him down with his .22.

I was crying against Papa's worn shirt. Papa smelled of dust and sweat, and I held on tight to his muscular frame. I must have been about four years old then. Papa reached in his pocket and gave me his clean handkerchief to wipe my face. He was always sharing his handkerchief with me, and I loved him for it. It had dried on the clothesline and still smelled like sunshine. It was soothing. I held it against my face, and my sobbing subsided.

"Are you upset with me, Corrie-girl, like the others?"

"I don't know, Papa, tell me why, again."

"Red killed five chickens in all. I tried to cure him of it, like I did our other dogs, but he was unwilling to change."

I remembered the drama of the last month. First, Papa had caught him just after he killed two hens. Papa had tied one of the hens around Red's neck and made him wear the hen like a collar until the bird had fallen apart. We all made a wide path around Red during that time. That had been enough to cure our old dog, Marshall, my favorite. He had learned his lesson and from then on was the hens' protector from the coyotes, raccoons, and foxes that prowled around at night, hoping for a raid on the coop.

Red did not learn, and about two weeks later, he was caught playing with a chicken he had just killed. I knew my papa disliked the idea, but he had heard about whacking the dog with the dead chicken for a lesson. My papa was determined, and I looked away as he did the task. My mama and brothers looked at Papa with disdain.

"What an old fool," my oldest brother Theo said. "I'll just tie Red up for a while, and that'll do the trick."

"Don't call him that! You're the fool!" I ran over and stomped as hard as I could on Theo's toe.

"You little brat!" he yelled and yanked me up by my ear. "You think you're special, don't you? We'll see how you like this."

He dragged me over to the water trough and dunked my head in. He held me there for what seemed like a minute. My arms flailed, searching for a way to pull myself out.

"Knock it off, you big bully!"

It was my older sister Marcia, and she had pushed Theo away in a surprising show of strength. Marcia was the sickly one, who usually kept to herself. We had never had much to do with each other.

"You better stop playing Papa's favorite or who knows what they'll do to you. Go on now. Don't be underfoot."

She gave me a little shove and walked back to the house. I stayed outside until dark, long enough to dry off and think about what she had said.

Papa's favorite? I didn't know what Marcia had meant by that, although I had heard *them* say it among other things.

"Tattletale!"

"Snitch!"

"Goody two-shoes!"

My brothers looked at me with such contempt and disgust when they said these things, so I knew it must be something bad. It just made me want to be with Papa even more. Mama didn't stick up for me. I think she even approved of her boys teasing me. Papa was my haven, and I sought him during every waking hour.

Theo followed through. He found an old rope and kept Red tied to a post for several days. Then he had proudly strutted over and untied him.

"There you go, Red. Be smart now. If you touch another chicken, you'll be tied back up."

Red killed his last chicken that very day. There would be no more time for tying him to a post. Papa went straight for his .22.

"You can't do that! He's my dog!" Theo yelled. He walked over quickly, like he was going to stop Papa.

"Then you do it," Papa said and motioned to give Theo the gun. "A dog is worthless to us if we have to keep him tied up all the time."

Theo just dropped his head and walked into the house. Coward.

Mama yelled out, "If you shoot him, don't expect me to help raise any more puppies!"

Papa wasn't going to be bullied this time. He didn't waste any more words on Theo or Mama. He put a rope on Red and gently took him out toward the dump. He was kind, even with this dreaded task. The boys watched from a distance. Mama busied herself at the clothesline. I took the babies in the house and closed the door.

I heard the shot and then wandered out to find Papa. I started crying as I got close to him. Poor Papa. He stood there with his shoulders slumped. It was always him against the rest of *them*. Why couldn't my brothers be more like him?

"Tell me why again."

"I did everything I knew to keep Red away from the chickens. He just wouldn't learn. It's like he was stealing food from our table every time he killed a hen. His heart was hardened against any learning. It is sort of like Pharaoh in Egypt, during the time of Moses.

"'And the Lord hardened the heart of Pharaoh, and he hearkened not unto them.' Pharaoh repeatedly hardened his own heart against God's will for His people to be free from the slavery in Egypt. God finally gave Pharaoh over to his own rebellious desire, and his heart remained hardened right unto death. Red was a detriment to us as he was greedily taking the provisions we gave him and then stealing *our* food. I gave him every chance to change. God is, likewise, patient with us. He desires all people to choose to walk in fellowship with Him. But there are those people who enjoy the pleasures of life freely, yet they don't give thanks to the One who provided the very breath in their lungs. God finally gives them what they wanted all along— *a life without Him.* That short life without Him leads right into an eternity without Him. Make sure you watch out for those thankless people in life, Corrie. They are the worst kind. You yourself practice giving thanks to Him for all things. Don't allow your heart to be hardened."

* * *

What a strange time to recollect this memory of my papa and to hear his words so clearly. *Papa, come back!* My head was hidden in Mrs. Rawlings's apron, and I was clinging to her. In this manner, I had avoided witnessing the murder of Frank. He had been the most volatile and had been dispatched first. I understood a little more now. Frank had hardened his heart. He was a thankless person like Papa had warned about, and he had continued in a lawless pattern for too long.

I heard Mrs. Rawlings mutter, "Mmm hmm, soon he'll be cold as a wagon tire."

If I could go back, I would have stayed with my head in the apron. I would have brought back memories of my papa, and his wise and comforting words. But, instead, I had pushed myself clear of Mrs. Rawlings in a final act of panic.

Martin! Where's Martin?

I scanned the bridges for him. I saw Frank hanging from the smaller bridge over the slough, still and solitary. The bridge, not a juniper, was bearing fruit. There were many people milling about on the main bridge over the river. I still did not see the tall, slight frame of Calvin Hall.

I considered Mr. Hall again. He had allowed devotion to *Mary Joe* destroy his life, like a deadly parasite. Later, Mrs. Rawlings would explain that the vigilantes had, at first, left him slumbering on the hotel couch. Maybe the hymn-sing had allowed for peaceful sleep. But then they returned for him after the others had been hung. They had dragged him out, still half asleep in his long underwear, and thrown him over. No more regard for him than a stray limb. The fools had cut the rope too long, and Mr. Hall's feet had struck the rocks below. It grieved me then to hear that he had suffered a more brutal death. I heard the men had even considered hanging Mary and one of her daughters but maybe lost their nerve as the sun threatened to rise and expose their identities.

Back in the present, cowering by Mrs. Rawlings, I now searched for Martin. I spotted him, tall and motionless, as the captors near him appeared to be talking among themselves. Was that hesitation? Perhaps they were changing their minds! I allowed hope to bloom inside me. I saw one of them give Mr. Harden a stronger shove, and he fell to his knees. He put his hands up, as if in prayer.

"They will let him go!" I said to Mrs. Rawlings.

"No, they won't. They have vowed to be rid of them all."

One man halted the group to tie another knot in Martin's rope.

My knees went weak again. I should speak up, like I had before. No, I was only the snitch. Just like my brothers had said. I had started all of this when I spoke up about Pal. I was a coward. I saw them pushing Martin toward the edge, and images began flashing quickly through my mind.

* * *

There was Martin in the rhubarb patch, laughing eyes over his cup of sugar. In the schoolroom, his long legs crossed, resting on an empty chair. Eyes closed, head back on his arms, smiling, engrossed in the story Mr. Harden was reading to us. His tall frame running with the kids during recess, but then stooping to lift a little girl who had fallen. Then there was that day by Miss Esther's house. His dark hair shone in the sunlight, but it was his light *within* that shone in my eyes that day.

In him was life, and the life was the light of men.

That day, standing with me next to Pal, he had looked at me with a deep well of kindness. His hand brushed mine, and he spoke to me about using the light I had in me for good. I could do it now. I could speak up for him.

* * *

I was working up to a protest when everyone instantly fell silent.

There was Martin, head held high.

The men pushed him closer to the edge, and Martin turned his head toward the crowd.

Then there was more silence—hesitation—as the lynch mob froze behind him.

What should I say?

Martin tilted his head toward the sky.

A man's footsteps slowly pounded across the length of the bridge. He shoved the motionless men out of his way with one arm and swiftly shoved Martin over the side with the other.

"No!"

I felt my own life leaving me through that cry. A white light flashed through my head. Mercifully, I would never be able to recall the moment Martin's rope jerked taut.

Chapter 16
O Ye Dry Bones
1910

I didn't know where I was when I awoke to a bright morning. I was in bed, in a modest but beautiful room. The bed faced a big, open window, and the breeze gently tickled the lacy curtains within. A woman came through the door with a tray and shyly approached me.

"You must be Mary. I'm Maite Harrison, James's mother."

Her eyes were a lovely gray, and her dark hair was gathered at her neck. I had never seen a lovelier woman. She was like Mrs. Heins, although more of a natural beauty and not dressed as fancy. I wondered at my own appearance and felt ashamed.

"Just relax," she said as she gently placed her hand on my head. "You've been quite ill. You came down with a fever the day of your wedding, and James brought you straight here."

He was probably glad to be rid of me, I thought. Maybe he was already searching for a heartier wife.

"How long have I been here?"

"It's been four days. You gave us quite a scare. James had to take care of things at his own place, but he's been here to visit, most days. Would you like to try to sit up?"

She leaned over and arranged some pillows behind me. She smelled like lemon verbena. Then she helped me to sip from a cup of tea.

"Is that better, Mary?"

"I actually go by Corrie."

"Yes, James did mention that. I think he likes to call you Mary." She smiled at me.

I hadn't heard him call me anything yet.

"How do you feel?"

I'm not sure what it was that made me feel so at ease with Mrs. Harrison. Maybe it was her gentle manner or the obviously good care I had been given. I had rarely been in the presence of such a relaxed, kind-hearted woman.

"I feel a little weak, but good mostly. What was wrong with me?"

"The doctor called it hysteria. James said you almost toppled out of the wagon, and he was unsure of what to do for you. He can care for sick livestock all day, with such patience, but was quite unnerved about how to care for his wife." Mrs. Harrison giggled.

His wife. It was strange to be called that since I still did not even know James. I wondered what would happen next.

"I'd like to keep you a few more days, if you don't mind. It may be too much for you to make the trip to James's until you have your strength back. You don't mind me keeping you to myself a bit longer?"

Keeping me? I don't remember anyone ever wanting to keep me, except Papa. Of course, Henry did, too, but I'm not sure he was even human. People in my life had mostly been trying to get rid of me, especially the women.

"I would like that, Mrs. Harrison. Thank you."

"You can call me Maite." She pronounced her name My-Tay, and it sounded beautiful. "Where I'm from, my name is a form of Maria or Mary. Isn't that wonderful? We nearly have the same name. We can be like the two Marys, witnessing the empty tomb of Jesus—a glorious day! James is our only child, so I'm very pleased to now have a daughter."

I was pleased to share my name with this woman. Much better her than the Mary Hall of long ago! Joy welled up inside me, but I was afraid to let it show. I marveled at the pretty room I was in, with a woman who wanted me to stay. *She called me her daughter*. I fidgeted with the white woven blanket over me. How did she keep everything so lovely and clean in this dusty desert?

"I'm guessing this is all very strange to you? Getting married to a man you don't know and moving to a new home? It was the same way for me, over twenty years ago. I told my parents I'd rather die than marry the stranger, Mr. Harrison. Now I know it was the best thing that ever happened to me. I can tell you more about it, unless you're tired and want me to leave you to rest?"

I shook my head as I was very anxious to hear her story. She motioned for me to drink more of my tea.

"My people were from the Biscay area of Spain. My aitona, or grandfather, would try to describe its beauty to me. The ocean waters were an emerald green, with rain soaked cliffs all around. His family had been whalers. He'd throw his arms in the air, like this, to make a V, so I'd know what the whale's spray looked like. The spray came when the whales surfaced and blew out air. He said the whales were often bigger than ten horses lined up! My grandfather was one of the brave men who came to America to mine for gold. He thought he'd make a lot of money and then return home, but this land got into his blood.

"My grandfather became a sheepherder instead, and the owner would pay him with sheep. In this way, he built up his own business. He said, at first, these deserts were far too big and lonely for him, but the space allowed for hundreds and even thousands of sheep. He'd be out alone with the sheep for about five days at a time before a camp tender would come along with provisions. Then there would be another five days alone. In this way, he grew accustomed to the solitude and the desert, and then could never imagine returning to the more confined home country — no matter how beautiful it was."

He had become acquainted with solitude, with the desert. It was part of him, and it was part of me.

Maite continued with admiration in her eyes, "My grandfather's first weeks out there were filled with fear, but that fear gradually changed into a passion for the desert. There was a time when he spent two whole years out there—without going to town once! He eventually married the daughter of another Basque rancher, and they had three children. My father, Peter, was born last.

"Is your father still living?" I was surprised at my own interruption.

"Yes, he is. He lives here, in fact. You will get to meet him very soon," she smiled. "My mama died about five years ago, and then Papa moved here last year. Your house is their old house."

My house? This woman was offering me so much, and she didn't even know me. My heart started to beat rapidly. Surely, once they realized who I really was, they would send me on my way. I was just a lazy, disrespectful, sullen girl, practically guilty of murder. I felt so dirty compared to this picture of loveliness before me. My thoughts were making it hard to breathe, and a feeling of panic came over me.

"Oh dear. I'm so sorry. I think I've expected too much of you and overtired you." Maite tried to help me lie back down, but my arms and legs were thrashing.

"Will!" she cried out toward the door. "Please go for the doctor. She's having some sort of fit."

I briefly saw a tall, light-haired man in the doorway. He must be James's father, and he had a worried look on his face. He turned, and then, suddenly, James was there—like an explosion. He looked angry.

"What's going on, Mother? I gave strict orders for Mary to rest. Why are the curtains and windows open?"

James quickly slammed the windows shut and darkened the room. His actions distracted me from my panic, and I began to calm down. I was curious as to what this forceful man, my husband, would do next.

"I'm sorry, James, but she took a good turn this morning, and we were getting to know each other. I do think I might've overtired her."

"Leave me with her," he said abruptly.

Maite gathered the tray and quickly left the room. My eyes were adjusting to the dimmed room, and I tried to focus on James's face as he slammed the door and approached me.

"Relax, Mary," he said as he arranged the pillows under my head. He didn't touch me, but his arms and hands were very near, encircling me as he arranged my blanket. I smelled his bay rum aftershave. This man was a mystery, and I felt as if he were casting a spell over me. I felt comfortably warm and sleepy.

"My name is Corrie," I whispered.

"No. Maybe to others. But to me, you are Mary," he said as he tucked loose strands of hair behind my ear. His hand lingered for a second on the side of my face, and I held my breath. He abruptly stood up, strode to the window, and looked back at me.

"I'll come back for you in the morning. Tomorrow you are coming home."

He left the room, and I heard him discussing the matter with his mother. She was softly protesting, but his replies were commanding and precise.

"I'm coming back for my wife tomorrow," he said, and I heard a door open and shut.

Something told me I better enjoy this time of rest and Maite's hospitality while I could. I had been pampered very little in my life. Maybe only one other time . . . with Smithy . . . on our journey . . .

Chapter 17
Hear the Word of the Lord
1907

Smithy had mentioned to Mr. Heins that there would be a place of respite near Nut Mountain, and we were drawing near to it at the end of our fifth day. We had, surprisingly, spent much of that afternoon riding in comfortable silence. Back near Painted Point, Smithy had shared a multitude of insights that gave me much to think about.

I pondered the seemingly endless expanse of sage and the windmill that emerged, like a mirage, from the *big empty*. We had seen three windmills so far, and each was wooden. Metal windmills had not made it that far west. We stopped and let Smithy's team, Crow and Betty, have their fill of water that had been pumped into the wooden trough. There were several small leaks, and we had to be careful to not sink down into the mud. We splashed our faces, but Smithy told me to wait for a drink at Coyote Spring. A water snake escaped from our sight into the coarse grass-like plants growing alongside the tank. Smithy called the grass *horsetail*.

"You can scrub out your pans with it. This water hole will be a busy place soon. Now that it's spring, the ranchers will be driving their cattle out for summer grazing. Imagine thousands of cattle spread throughout these flats."

"That many? It doesn't seem like there's enough to eat out here."

"It is surprising, isn't it? The cattle don't just stay together in one big group, which would be a problem. They naturally break into smaller family groups, with maybe eight or so. The cattle are experts at browsing for different species of food. Their diet is very diverse. They eat the brush—like the horsebrush, rabbitbrush, and bitterbrush—and also the leaves they can reach of some of the hard-to-find deciduous trees. There's some grass, but they also eat wildflowers, such as the scarlet globe mallow—over there. The cattle are good stewards of the land. They don't eat the plants down to nothing. They'll take a few bites and then move on to a different food source . . ."

I was staring at the scarlet globemallow, and I didn't hear all that Smithy was saying. The flower was an unexpected flash of brilliant red in the middle of dry dust. It seemed a waste for such beauty in a place where nobody may ever see it. I could relate more to the dry dust than to the life coming out of it.

"Some call that *cowboy's delight* as it must be a relief to the eyes." Smithy had followed my gaze. "How amazing that something so pretty would show itself amid what looks like deprivation. But it really isn't deprived. Our loving Father gave it everything it needs to survive and thrive out here. He enjoys its beauty even if no one else ever sees it. And the animals do enjoy it as food. The antelope and rabbits and many others eat it, too."

Even Solomon in all his glory was not arrayed like one of these.

Papa had told me about the flowers and how God had clothed them in splendor. Why had I not remembered that before? *Everything it needed.* I thought on this as we made our way toward Nut Mountain. My mind seemed trained to always dwell on the negative, on the things I had felt deprived of. Like my years at Mrs. Rawlings's, which had felt so bleak and empty. Could it be that I had received everything I needed—even if I'd felt neglected? Could beauty spring forth from the dust that had been my life? If the loving Father Smithy talked about enjoyed the flowers, did He enjoy me? Could I be of some use for something? That globemallow seemed to have more purpose than I did. The problem was, I did not know how to make my life beautiful or how to be useful.

"Here is Coyote Spring, and the Thatchers live just over there."

I gazed over at an area that was greener than our surroundings. That must be the area of the spring. Out here, every spring was vital for supporting life, and thus many of them had small living quarters built nearby. It was lovely to see wild irises growing along the marshy area, but I was not thrilled at the prospect of meeting the Thatchers. I was quite comfortable with Smithy as my only companion.

"Can't we just stock up on water and then continue on?"

"It'll be all right, Corrie. I want you to experience Mrs. Thatcher's good hospitality. She is an Indian, a Pit River Indian, actually."

A Pit River Indian? Like Mary Hall?

Now, I was really nervous and not wishing to stop. Would she be like her?

"Hello, the house!"

Smithy called out to alert the Thatchers of our presence. It was a few minutes before an old, stooped man wandered out first. His clothes were worn, like him, but had been kept neatly mended. He walked slowly up to Crow, put his hand out, and whispered a greeting to him. He did the same for Betty. His manner was unhurried, and he finally turned to us to offer a mostly-toothless smile.

"You took your time showing yourself, Smithy. We've missed you."

"I've missed you, too, Stu. Is Mrs. Thatcher well?"

"She's fine. Just rushing to double the soup now that we have company. We'll go inside in a moment. She will not believe her eyes when she sees this girl. And you are?"

Mr. Thatcher was standing near me now, with his hand outstretched toward me. I offered my hand to him then, more easily than I offered words.

"This is Corrie. She's riding with me from Alturas to Denio. We've been having an easy and pleasant journey, and I've been looking forward to her meeting you." Smithy smiled at me encouragingly.

"Nice to meet you, Mr. Thatcher." He was still holding my hand and smiling up at me. He was easily eighty years old.

"It's a pleasure to meet you, too. Why don't you climb down and get a drink from our spring? There's no water finer or smoother-tasting than this here."

I climbed down and followed Mr. Thatcher to the covered wooden box. He knelt down, slid the cover off, and reached in with a metal soup ladle. He offered it up to me for a drink. I looked at Smithy, and he nodded for me to try it. I don't know why I closed my eyes while I drank, but I did. The water was cold, but so smooth going down. I saw Martin before me then.

* * *

Martin and I had neared a seasonal creek, not far from school. We had sneaked away for a little hike during recess and had easily lost track of time. It was early spring still, and a beautiful time in the valley around Lookout. We never could've guessed the darkness that would soon fall over everything. It would never be the same again.

Martin knelt down and cupped his hands to drink. I mimicked him and did the same. The water was so cold, and it awakened my senses.

"It's safe to drink here now, Corrie, but once it gets too much warmer, you won't want to be drinking it. The cows haven't been grazing above here yet. Doesn't it make you feel alive? You can just taste the *life* in this water."

The water that I shall give him shall be in him a well of water springing up into everlasting life.

A well of water springing up.

I liked the words, and I repeated them in my mind. We drank and then washed our faces with it. I surprised myself by giving Martin a little splash. He cupped more water and slowly released it over my head. I could feel every drop of icy water as it slid down my head and neck and back. It made me shudder, and I felt energized. I laughed and ran after Martin. He was able to dodge around me, but then I turned quickly and grabbed him. I held on tight around his waist and looked up at him. He hugged me back just for a moment, but then his expression turned serious. Martin's arms dropped to his side. I buried my face in his chest. I hadn't hugged anyone like this since my papa long ago, and I didn't want to let go. His strong frame reminded me so much of Papa. Martin gave my head an awkward pat and gently started to pry my arms apart.

"What's going on here? Wait until Willa hears of this."

Mrs. Howard stood there with her son, Charlie, who held a bucket. I did not understand her disapproving gaze or the sneer on Charlie's face. Within a day, Mrs. Howard had told Mrs. Rawlings and most everyone in town. I was warned to keep away from Martin after that. His expression was sad whenever I glanced at him across the schoolroom. Mr. Harden had been told that we could not sit near one another. He hadn't done anything wrong. It was my fault—I had been the one to hug him.

* * *

Charlie Howard was seventeen years old and had been a friend of Martin's since they were young. Charlie had preferred the innocent fun of young boys to the sinister pranks of the older boys like Frank and Jim. When Frank and Jim's pranks grew more serious, and when Yantis came to town, Charlie's father had poisoned his mind even against Martin. Charlie started to keep his distance and even tried to pick fights with Martin. Martin mourned the friendship in silence. Charlie's father would become one of the lynch mob's ringleaders. Charlie must have wanted his father's approval, and he went along with the mob, getting caught up in the frenzy. Then, he had stood passively next to his father and the others as Martin was pushed off of the bridge. The guilt must have quickly consumed him. That same morning, as the town was first waking up to the bodies hanging heavy at the bridge, Charlie had galloped away on his father's horse. He hadn't been heard from since. In fact, each of the men involved showed their guilt in various ways, some by going crazy. Many felt that their families were cursed thereafter.

* * *

There at Coyote Spring, my tears welled up again as I drank in the life of that water. The memory of Martin faded. I was just as guilty of Martin's death as Charlie was, and maybe my life would always be cursed. I quickly wiped away the tears before anyone could notice.

"Nothing like it, is there, Corrie?" Smithy asked me. "The minerals in the water give it the smooth taste."

I nodded weakly and handed the ladle back to Mr. Thatcher.

"Come inside now and meet my Chrissy."

I was nervous and weak and could barely move. What was wrong with me? Was it because his wife was a Pit River Indian that I was feeling this way? Maybe meeting any woman made me nervous. Smithy gently pulled my hand and led me toward the small cabin. We went through a doorway covered with a blanket and were met with the smell of smoke and onions. It took my eyes a moment to adjust to the dim interior. I saw Mrs. Thatcher stooped over a little woodstove in the corner. She was stirring the contents of a pot. She couldn't have been even five feet tall. She was preciously small. She looked over at me, and her eyes smiled. Did I even see her eyes in her wrinkled face, or was it the wrinkles around her eyes that smiled? She shuffled over to me and cupped my face in her hands. Her palms were pleasantly cool, smooth, and dry, like my papa's handkerchiefs. She smiled up at me and then put her arms around me with such love and tenderness. I don't know why it happened, but I just started quietly sobbing. How could such a little woman have that power over me? She whispered soothingly as I cried. Mrs. Thatcher smelled like dust and onions, and all that is good.

"My girl, it is done. There is no going back. Just today now, only today."

How did she know to say those words to me? She cupped my face again and wiped my tears. She shuffled softly to the stove and dipped a cloth in one of the pots. She squeezed out the extra water, waited a moment for it to cool, and then bathed my face in the warmth. Then she surprised me by giving it a good scrubbing. I almost cried out, but then laughed in spite of myself. I simply wasn't used to that much attention. Mrs. Thatcher laughed, also, softly talking and giving her pot a stir every now and then. I sat down, hypnotized by her movements. The men were sitting, also, as they hadn't made a peep since we came in. I have since learned that a woman's fussing care has a calming and healing effect to all who experience it.

"Thank you," I finally managed.

"You're happy to have a young one here, aren't you?" Mr. Thatcher smiled. "We were never able to have children, and your being here is a gift to her."

He called me a gift.

Mrs. Thatcher smiled at me and brought over a bowl of soup. The blend of smells was intoxicating, and I started to take a bite.

"No, no, no," she said, and I almost dropped my spoon.

"First, we'll say *thanks*." She closed her eyes and lifted her hands to the ceiling. "Heavenly Father, thank you for bringing me this child. Please heal her from the sorrows I see in her eyes. Give her *joy*. Thank you for this meal and for our Smithy."

Mrs. Thatcher handed bowls to her husband and to Smithy. "Better than hard boiled eggs!"

We all laughed then.

She made a motion with her hands to hurry up and eat. I ate the soup and felt the goodness go all the way to my soul. She also brought out some sourdough bread. It was delicious. Mrs. Thatcher watched me to see my reaction, and she smiled.

"I will show you how to make it," she said, pointing to the bread.

So we stayed. That is what happens with good hospitality. It is like coming home, and one hour turns into several, and then soon it has been days. I had decided, the moment she held me in her arms, that it would take a pack of mules to drag me away. This place felt like a real home. This was my new *womb*, and I would relish in it. I would embrace each moment of protection and love, fully knowing that no one can stay in a womb forever. The labor pains would come. A forced exit was always around the corner for me.

Chapter 18
Breath
1910

Maite's presence brought me serenity, just as Mrs. Thatcher's had. But James was coming for me tomorrow, and Maite and I had to take advantage of our time together. James had blown in and out earlier, like a summer storm, and it was still only late morning. He had given me such a shock that whatever fit I was having was long forgotten. I felt calm when I woke up after a deep nap. Maite had promised to teach me a game from her home country.

"The game is called Mus, which is a variation of our word for 'kiss.'" She raised her eyebrows at me and laughed softly. "Usually it takes four to play, but I think I can at least teach you the gist of it."

Her fingers were long and elegant and lily-white as she shuffled the cards. I hid my tan, work-worn hands under the blanket.

"There are four rounds to the game—grande, chica, pares, and juego—and each round has its own rules. If we were in pairs, we would discuss our cards with our partners before deciding if we will make a bid or pass. It's a very verbal game."

"Yes, and Maite is the master at bluffing." The man I assumed to be Will Harrison had walked in and was smiling at his wife. He stood behind her and gave her shoulders a little squeeze. "Play Mus with Maite at your own risk. Good morning, Mary. I am Will, James's father. It's such a pleasure to meet you."

He held his hand out and took mine in his. I immediately gathered that he was a kind and gentle man, although he had called me Mary. I was relieved that he had distracted us from the game. I had very little experience with games, and one that required a lot of talking would've been torture. I would rather fade into the white of my blanket than to have to compete against my bold and expressive mother-in-law. I smiled gratefully at Will.

"Our son convinced you to move to Dry Valley, did he? Well, I'm not surprised. James always gets what he sets his sights on." There was no resentment in his expression. If anything, he seemed in awe of his son.

"He reminds me of his father," Maite added, winking at me.

"I don't think so, dear. His temperament definitely comes from the Larralde side." He gave her a kiss on her cheek. "Good day, for now. Get some rest, Mary. James always keeps his word, so I imagine he'll be here for you at first light."

"That's my Will. Isn't he a gem? I guess it's true—James takes more after his Grandpa Pete. Will manages to get a lot done, but he operates at a different speed than the Larraldes. Will was made to rule over his land and cattle. James seems more designed to command an army—may it never be so." Maite clasped her hands.

A knot formed in my stomach at the shadow of sorrow that passed quickly over Maite's face. It obviously pained her to even think of losing her only child. I was surprised at the feeling since I had not formed any attachment to James. I was even oblivious to the pain of war. For the older generations, though, the Civil War had touched every corner of the United States, and they usually avoided the talk of war entirely.

"My papa's uncle died in the war. He was young—more like an older brother to my father. They say Andere was brave and handsome! His parents were angry and heartbroken when he left to volunteer and fight. He had come over to start a new life in America, but he was drawn to fighting. The Spanish Civil War had been so devastating to my people, and then he wanted to go fight for a country that was new to him! Fighting was in his blood, I guess. This is why I worry about James. He is drawn to conflict. Maybe he takes after Andere."

I listened to Maite talk of my new family and of this vehement man who was my husband. I was feeling a bit of admiration toward him. It was like watching a storm roll over the desert toward you. You realize the destruction that lies within, but you stand immobilized, mesmerized by the beauty of its strength.

"Will's right, and I should let you rest. Mus will have to wait for another time. James will come early, and I suppose I'll have to give you up. Well, I will let you settle in at the home place, but then I will pay you a visit, eh? Do you think a visit in two weeks would be proper?"

"That'd be wonderful." *But two whole weeks? That seemed like an eternal amount of time. What will I do with myself? With James?*

Maite read my worried expressions and said, "Just take it one day at a time, dear. I remember when I first came here with Will. I hear he had his eye on me for years. He had even built this house in anticipation of our marriage. You would think I would've prepared myself in all that time to leave my own family. No, I was still terrified and homesick for my mother. You probably miss your mother, too?"

I gave her a blank stare. My mother? I had lost track of the last time I had given her a thought, let alone ever missed her. Was she even living? How could I feel homesick for someone who had turned on me at such a young age?

"I don't know my mother," I finally said without expression.

Maite drew a breath and clasped my hands with hers. "Oh, you poor child. Not know your own mother? I'm so sorry. I can't even imagine. God brought you to me now, and I'll care for you. You can ask me anything. You better think quick though, eh? Tomorrow's the big day." She smiled, squeezed my hands, and then gave them a kiss.

"What if he doesn't like me?"

"Who? James?" She laughed. "James doesn't make mistakes. If he didn't like you, he wouldn't have married you. He's a discerning man. He can read people right away. I think he is quite taken with you—I can tell by how nervous and agitated he's been acting. Don't worry, deep down he's very faithful and kind. He had his eye on you. He made up his mind to love you a long time ago."

I did not remember ever seeing him before, but Aunt Ruth had seen him. She knew that he was a prospect willing to cart me away. But Henry, on the other hand, he had caught my attention. Sweet Henry, not of this world. I didn't want to start thinking of him because I was stuck in reality now. Chest deep in it, actually. There was no escaping it. I had a long night of thinking ahead of me, and Henry could not be a part of it. I needed to contemplate how I was going to cope with being a wife to James.

Maite wrapped a shawl around my shoulders and said, "When Will brought me here, I was such a mess! He thought all his dreams had come true when we said our vows, but he didn't know that I was still so much like a child. I loved my parents, and I cried for many days after our wedding. But, you see, Will is a patient man. He'd put his arm around me and talk kindly to me. He gave me a lot of time to mourn. What a spoiled brat I was! I'm sorry, but I do not think James is that long-suffering."

"I rarely cry, and I won't be homesick for anyone."

"That's good. You're a stronger girl than I am. You'll be just right for James. And remember, I'll come in two weeks, eh?" She laughed and then whispered, "Perhaps, eventually, you'll call me Mama."

Mama.

I would look forward to her visit. I fell asleep easier than I expected, and the night passed quickly. The comfort of the bed had won over my worried thoughts. In the morning, I heard a door slam. Fast footsteps approached, bringing me with a rush to the task at hand.

"Are her things packed, Mother?"

"Yes, of course. Will you allow me to help her dress?"

"I can manage. Leave us."

I caught a glimpse of Maite, lovely, retreating in her nightgown, her hair flowing.

James came close and looked at me with concern. He touched my face briefly, and I let him gather me in his arms. He sat me up on the side of the bed.

"Mary, it's time to go. Here, let's slip this over your gown."

I still felt weak, and my efforts were feeble. James was all business as he awkwardly fastened the dress over my other gown. It took him quite a while to button my shoes. Finally, he gathered me and my bag all up into one load. Our exit down the hall and outside was quick and blurred. I never knew such a fast walker. James barely allowed Maite to kiss my cheek before he had me bundled up in the wagon.

"Remember, James, she's still recovering. Be patient with her. She's like a lost girl. I will pay her a visit in a couple of weeks. Please let me know how she's doing . . ."

Maite's voice faded in the distance as James prompted his horse and left without a wave.

"Are you warm enough, Mary?" He hugged me to him with his free arm.

I nodded then scooted away from him and stared ahead in silence. I was thinking of the way he was insisting on calling me *Mary*. It made me loathe my own skin. The only *Mary* I had ever known personally was Mary Hall. The Indian Mary, who had brought down everyone around her. The one who had barely escaped the noose.

* * *

I remember her coming by Mrs. Rawlings's house from time to time to try to sell us eggs. Mrs. Rawlings had chickens of her own, so the answer was always *no*. There was no man at our house for her to flirt with, but she had other intentions. Mary Hall had seen Martin and me laughing together, and she did not like it. I spoke with contempt the last time she came to the door to try to sell eggs.

"Are you slow? I've told you at least five times that we have our own chickens and don't need your eggs."

Mary spat at me then.

"You don't own anything. Orphan trash. I'll tell Martin to stay away or his brothers will make him pay." She had kept her eyes on me as she slowly walked around the corner.

I hated her. My papa had warned me about harboring bitterness.

Follow peace with all men, and holiness, without which no man shall see the Lord.

* * *

I was in big trouble. I was still harboring unforgiveness against too many people. My brothers, Mrs. Rawlings, all those who killed Martin . . . *me*. I could follow that root of bitterness still deeper. Like a mesquite bush, which is impossible to dig up intact. My bitter root went all the way back to the source of my life, my mother. Once you think ill of your own flesh, you can find fault with just about anyone. How would I be able to stand James calling me *Mary* when all it did was bring forth such hateful thoughts?

"Please don't call me that. My mother called me that, and I don't think kindly of her."

"You are Mary to me, and I'll remind you to honor your father and mother."

"My father is long dead, and my mother probably is, too."

"You should be thankful that they brought you into this world."

"This world has been nothing but trouble to me."

"I won't abide by such thankless talk."

James was quiet then, and I was struck dumb by his direct words. There was no idle chatter with this man. Unlike Smithy, who carried on a one-sided, melodious conversation, James had a use for each and every word. His abrupt nature was drawing out parts of me I had never shown before—

"Then you may as well take me back to Denio. You won't find an ounce of thankfulness in me. Either take me back, or enjoy the silence."

"I don't mind silence."

We rode on in that manner for the remainder of the distance. We had traveled out of Dry Canyon into what looked like endless sagebrush flats, but then we suddenly dropped down into a green creek basin.

"This is Mud Creek and our home."

Home.

I grew weak at the thought and had to rely on James more than I wanted to help me from the wagon. When had I ever called a place *home*? I had felt at home at the Thatcher's near Nut Mountain and at Maite's. But to have my own home was a foreign experience.

James carried me through the door and deposited me down on a wooden bench inside.

"Sit here while I unharness the team."

Did he think I was going to run off? He was actually right to worry. If I weren't so weak, I might have. I was scared to death. How was I going to keep a house and be his wife, too? I was too incompetent and self-absorbed. I didn't have a nurturing bone in my body. I could probably manage to care for a child, but that was straightforward—I had been around enough of them. Making a man happy seemed like an unsolvable mystery. And James seemed so demanding. Now, Henry would have been a different story. He would have pampered me. He would have been patient and kind and understanding. James didn't care to understand me at all, and he would probably expect a hot meal as soon as he came back.

I put my hand on the wall and managed to stand up. I shuffled to the door and waited a moment to catch my breath. I saw a tree in the distance and decided I could make it. James would be better off without me. He could find a sweet little wife to do his bidding with a song in her heart. I probably made it three steps before I collapsed.

"Mary, you're like a foolish child. What gave you the idea? You would've been coyote food by nightfall." James was carrying me back to the house.

"You don't want me. I don't know the first thing about being a wife to you."

"You'll learn."

James laid me on the bed and pulled a quilt, fashioned from denim, up to my chin. He stood with his face over me, eyes steady, and then leaned down close. He held it there for what seemed like minutes. I was holding my breath, unsure of what was about to happen.

"Please rest," he finally whispered, close to my ear, and then walked out into the other room.

His breath on me left me a little shaken. Through the doorway, I watched him walk over to a stove. The house was spare and aged, but well-tended. Harnesses and clothes hung on hooks along the bedroom wall. The room smelled of leather and bay rum. It was all very manlike, save for some curtains that his grandmother most likely made. James came back with a bowl of beans.

"These beans should strengthen you. I imagine, in no time, you will have us better fed."

"I don't cook."

Now, that was a straight-up lie. It would have been more truthful to tell him not to expect me to cook, as the sooner he tired of me, the better. I had learned how to cook well enough from both Mrs. Rawlings and Aunt Ruth, but only when I was forced. I had also learned to make Mrs. Thatcher's sourdough bread—but I haven't told you that part of the story, yet.

The truth was, I was terribly lazy. Remember the books at Aunt Ruth's? I would rather read away a day. My other pastime was standing outside listening to the desert. Like the moment Henry appeared. Years before, the cows had been my lazy-day companions. James had no idea how inept I was. I would not serve any good purpose. I recalled a sentence I had read out of Smithy's Bible, the one day I attempted to read it in Denio. I had not gotten very far—I was mostly skimming through it—but I read that God wanted Adam to have a help meet. Those were straightforward enough words, *help meet*. Adam wasn't complete until God gave him Eve. She would meet every need that he could not fulfill on his own. James was definitely a man, and there must be something he was lacking since he came to fetch me from Aunt Ruth's. But he and I clashed. Destruction, not help, would be the end result.

"You'd be better off taking me back to Denio. There was a man named Henry there who loved me just the way I am. He didn't ask me to cook or do anything else. I need to go back and wait for him."

I heard a loud thud and realized that my foolishness had gone too far. James came rushing back in the room, and his face was dark red. His eyes were lit more than usual, and he squeezed my arm.

"We were married before God, and I'll not tolerate another word about any other."

He held my gaze steadily for a moment, released my arm, walked out, and slammed the door.

I stubbornly made up my mind . . . *Nothing to worry about, James. You won't hear another word out of me . . .*

Chapter 19
You Shall Live
1907

I had made up my mind to live forever with the Thatchers at Coyote Spring, and I had let Smithy know. I told him the Thatchers would no doubt like to keep me since they didn't have any children of their own, and I was still working up the courage to ask them. Smithy had followed me on one of my foraging expeditions, and he was making an appeal to my stubborn nature.

"Corrie, I promised Mr. Heins that I'd get you to Denio safely," he said, using his sternest tone and turning me around so he could look me in the eye. "We have already stayed here longer than I intended. Your Aunt Ruth is short on help, and you need to be of service to her."

"But I've never felt more at home, and the Thatchers could use my help."

"I agree that it's very nice here, and I know you appreciate the hospitality. We can stay a few more days, but beyond that, people may start to worry about us."

I was enamored with Mrs. Thatcher, so tiny yet lively, and followed her wherever she went. She would slip out in the early morning hours, before the men were awake, taking her .22 rifle. She would often bring back fresh game and any edible plants she had collected. Her favorites were the early desert dandelion greens and the mesquite pod beans which were a bit harder to find. She had to walk very far to find the mesquite. She would also harvest the mesquite leaves, bark, and roots to treat various ailments.

It was exhilarating and delightful to be out at first light—to witness the constant shuffle of jackrabbits and pygmy rabbits around sagebrush. I was fortunate to glimpse one roadrunner, somehow humanlike in its determination to get to a particular destination and never relaxing to take in the view. My favorite creature to see and hear was the Bell's sparrow. They also darted around sagebrush with their "tik tik" chatter and bell-like chirps. It was mating season, and all the desert creatures were busy, noisy, pursuing.

"Are you and Mr. Thatcher hiding from someone out here, Mrs. Thatcher?" I asked her on one of our outings.

"Please call me Chrissy now. Mrs. Thatcher sounds too fancy!" She chuckled. "You could say that we're hiding from something, not someone. We grew weary of the many conflicts between the Indians, ranchers, and the cavalry. Life is too brief to spend it in anger, jealousy, and unforgiveness. It consumed them all. Their vision was narrowed, and their ears plugged up. Not Stu and me. We have so much love and thankfulness! This opens our eyes wide to beauty, kindness, providence! Our ears can hear each creature's song of praise. We prefer to live out here in fellowship with His Creation."

She was lovely—bathed in the morning's rays. Her smile was glorious. I thought about what she said. They had chosen to move here and leave the turmoil behind them. Couldn't I choose to live here and leave my turmoil behind? So far, I kept dragging my hurts along with me and could only forget them for short lengths of time. I reasoned that if I could stay with the Thatchers for a long time, I would become like them.

As promised, Chrissy showed me how to make a sourdough starter for bread. It was nearly as natural as breathing.

"First, mix a little water and a little flour to make a wet dough. You're doing fine. Next, I'll have you take it outside for a couple of days, keeping it covered with a towel. Once in a while, when you go outside, give the dough a little stir. You'll catch the natural yeast that floats unseen." She waved her hands around in the air. "When many bubbles appear, you'll know it's ready. It means there's *life*!"

That was the perfect job for me, escaping outside to catch the wild yeast. I removed the towel and gave the dough a number of exaggerated stirs, twirling myself around with the tilted bowl as I imagined harnessing the unseen elements in the air. I felt very young again, and I missed the twins. This job would have given us the giggles.

After two days, the dough was dotted with little bubbles and had a slight sour smell to it.

"You did it!" Chrissy said with a grin. "The rest is easy—add a little more flour and water and some salt. Stir it and let it sit until evening."

When evening came, we didn't even have to knead the dough. We just dumped it into the pan and baked it in their homemade wood-burning oven. The whole process was peaceful and easy, unlike my days of punching and kneading massive amounts of dough with Mrs. Rawlings. I had carried around a sense of imminent failure ever since my pie crust disaster. In contrast, Chrissy exuded calm, without the constant fretting.

"Cast your cares on Jesus, girl. There's nothing that He can't handle for you. Stop carrying around those burdens."

I surprised myself by giving her a spontaneous hug. I felt lighter then, momentarily shaking off the heavy darkness that cloaked me. Things would be okay if I could just stay with the Thatchers, I thought.

All the days there were just right with the small yet productive chores that *nourished and protected*. The stories and laughter after supper *warmed and embraced*. Some evenings, we would even sing together, *strengthening*. When the conversation faded, we slept where we lay, and I was *comforted* by the noises of my slumbering friends. I felt I had returned to the *womb.* By the time I was released from it, I felt I would be fully developed—ready to face the world.

That was a nice dream while it lasted. But remember the forced exit I warned you about, the one that always comes for me? This time, it came as a pain in Smithy's side. He ignored it at first and smiled his way through the day. Maybe he didn't want to leave, either. Pretty soon, it was too hard for him to ignore. I think he didn't want to worry the Thatchers, so he just told them it was time to move on.

"I made a promise to get Corrie to Denio, and as a supply man, I like to keep my word."

I was childish then in the way I pleaded with him and tried various ploys to stay longer. I even ran off and hid in the desert—until Chrissy sought me out.

"You need to respect Smithy's authority. He's a good man, a man of God. He'll care for you and teach you. Come back with me now."

Chrissy's words and the pained expression on Smithy's face finally stopped my antics. After an hour or so, Smithy and I rolled away.

When their place was out of sight, Smithy told me, "I think I'm dying."

"What do you mean? Chrissy is as good as a doctor. Let's go back!" I was frantic. I surprised myself by trying to wrench the reins from his hands. His hands felt clammy.

"No, Corrie! This is different. She wouldn't be able to help. I was making squaw tea and taking other herbs back there, but the relief was only temporary. I promised to get you to Denio. We'll need to go as fast as the horses will take us."

"Do something else then! You're the one who told me about all of God's healing herbs. Find one to help you!"

"When it's my time, it's my time. There's nothing on this earth that'll change that. I'm not scared."

But I was scared. Smithy was no longer my carefree companion. There was no comforting chatter or eating of eggs. His complexion was frighteningly gray. He merely looked ahead as we rode, keeping the horses going at the quickest walk the road allowed.

I started to cry. I would probably never see Chrissy again, and Smithy was desperately ill. My quiet tears gave way to gut-wrenching sobs. I was pathetic and selfish. Even with his pain, Smithy tried to comfort me, but there were no words that could soothe me. He patted my back and tried to smooth my hair.

I wore myself out and lay down on the seat—my head on Smithy's leg. I slept for a time and woke with fear. Smithy was involuntarily moaning.

"The pain is bad, Corrie. I'm going to stop. Would you please brew a little of the squaw tea?"

I jumped down and found the dried cluster of ephedra twigs. I started the fire preparations but looked over to see Smithy doubled over, vomiting. I dropped everything and ran to him. When I put my arms around him, I could feel that he was burning with fever. I grabbed a blanket, threw it on the ground, and helped lower him onto it. He was shaking with chills and groaning. My face was wet with tears, but I told myself to not lose control again. Smithy's abdomen looked bloated, and he didn't want me to touch it.

I loosened his belt and told him, "We'll stay here tonight, and then tomorrow I'm taking you back to Chrissy's."

"No, I won't allow it. Time to grow up, Corrie. If we go back, you'll never leave. Look." Smithy weakly lifted his arm and pointed in a northeasterly direction, past a group of tabletops and mahogany ridges. "Memorize those mountains. God has a plan for you—that way. No matter what, take the horses in that direction until you get to Denio Station. The path is well-worn."

I took his hand and pressed it to my wet face. "No, Smithy. I can't do it without you. You're my family now, and I want to stay with you."

"Now, listen. You have brought me so much joy. Be thankful for your time with me, and with Chrissy. Never forget it. It'll be like a secret treasure you can keep in your heart forever. But you have to keep going in the race that's been set before you. You have more growing to do. You can't just go hide at Nut Mountain. Your aunt needs you, and I have to keep my promise to get you there. You're a strong girl, and God has made you that way for a reason."

I didn't want to be strong, and I sure didn't feel strong. Despite my best efforts, I was losing control again. I wept openly and lay my head down next to his.

"I have come to love you, Corrie, but there's One who loves you even better."

I lifted my head with a start. Those were the same words my father had said that last day I was with him.

"What do you mean, Smithy? Papa said those same words to me. He never finished saying them."

"God loves you, Corrie. The same God who made you has a love for you that is far greater than any human love. Human love is fickle. Seek Him until you find Him. I won't be able to go any further, but you must promise me that you'll go to your aunt. Everything of mine will now be yours. Take my Bible. It is my most treasured earthly possession, and I want it to be yours."

I nodded my head weakly and lay back down next to him. He put his arm over me, and he started murmuring. I believe he was praying. I was comforted, and I quickly gave in to my exhaustion. You will not be surprised to hear that Smithy succumbed to his ailment during the night. I awoke, shivering in the cool desert morning, to find his arm still over me. Even in the throes of death, he did not abandon his effort to comfort me.

I was out of tears again and shed no more for him. Rather, I numbly yet lovingly went through the motions of caring for his remains. I wrapped him in his blanket, not thinking that he would've rather me keep it for the cold nights ahead. There was not an abundance of rocks around, so I had to find a soft bank of dirt that I could easily push over the top of him. I hoped that a stream of water would not come too soon and push him away. Smithy wouldn't care—he placed no value on his empty shell. By now, he had surely found the reward he spoke so highly of.

I grabbed his well-worn Bible, feeling that I should speak some words over him. I just opened it and read the first thing I saw.

It was in Isaiah and was fittingly dramatic. "Oh that thou wouldest rend the heavens, that thou wouldest come down, that the mountains might flow down at thy presence." I raised my voice louder with each word and then skimmed ahead to what caught my fancy. "But now, O Lord, thou art our father; we are the clay, and thou our potter; and we all are the work of thy hand."

I was satisfied then that Smithy would have approved of that tribute.

I spoke lovingly, as he would have, to Betty and Crow, apologizing that I had left them harnessed all night. I gathered the few items I had scattered the night before and put them in the wagon. I decided to dump out the rest of Smithy's hard-boiled eggs. That is probably what killed him, I thought.

I took a deep breath. Then, seated there in Smithy's seat on the wagon, I looked back toward Chrissy's and then to the northeast, the mahogany ridges. I considered my choice for a moment. I could easily head back to that *womb*, the place of solace. But it was Smithy's burial day, I finally reckoned, and no matter my own feelings, I would not disobey him.

"Betty and Crow, you know what to do. You heard him as well as I did. Go on now."

Chapter 20
Sinews
1910

It is the toughest of tissues that tie muscles to bone and unite into a singular purpose. I could be made of tough material when I set my mind to it. My determination served me well back in the desert with Betty and Crow, but James was not as compliant. It was as if he could see straight into my soul and then was disappointed with what he found.

"I don't mind silence, but I see a root of rebellion in you. I won't force-feed you, so I suppose hunger will be your consequence."

He had left me in the bed, and I could catch glimpses of him moving about that night and in the early morning. He was fastidious about his schedule and appearance. He had made his breakfast preparations at night and then was up and dressed just before first light. I couldn't see where he slept, maybe on the floor in the other room. After splashing his face with water and giving it a good scrub, he glanced over at me.

"Mary, you'll find the chamber pot at the end of the bed, and it is time for you to get up. I think you are well enough to take care of your necessities. I believe my mother was pampering you."

I considered, for a moment, whether I would survive two weeks like this before Maite would come for her visit. It was doubtful. I was already weak from my illness, and my body was desperate for sustenance. If I didn't eat soon, I would probably go downhill fast.

That was my decision—life or death. I turned my face to the wall and away from James.

I was in a strange mental state. Memories flashed as clear as day, both happy and sad.

* * *

Looking up, I saw the towering, sturdy frame of my father in the barnyard at first light. He looked back and smiled, scooping me up in his arms.

"You see those mama cows, Corrie? They'll be calving any day, and I tell you what, I'm going to name one after my girl."

But suddenly, I was taller and reached out to squeeze the chubby cheeks of the twins as they stared up at me with glee. What happened to their playful older sister? My brothers were in the background calling me an old maid.

"Who'd want to marry a broomstick?" they laughed.

"Some girls just aren't fit for marrying or childbearing," Mama answered them. "I think your sister might be one of them. There is nothing soft or affectionate about her."

Then I was running from Mama, Mrs. Rawlings, and her children—toward Martin, whose face was interchanging with that of Henry, but the smile was the same . . . playful, thoughtful, loving.

"Corrie, run with me! Grab my hand. No one will find us there." Their laughter faded. Of course it did—they were both gone. As final as the end of the rope. I saw it then, swaying slowly, and Martin's body slicing the morning light.

* * *

"No, no, no!" I screamed and fell from the bed to the floor. I clawed the rough, wooden floor, screaming and sobbing. My fingers were soon raw and bloody.

James ran to me and tried to contain my thrashing.

I shifted in his arms and wanted to hit him.

He turned me over and pinned me to the floor. He sat on me and held my arms back above my head. I twisted, trying to get away.

"What is it? You've gone mad."

I weakened, looking up into his eyes. He looked stern, but I was surprised to see worry in his eyes. His eyes were so light against his dark hair and mustache, and they were captivating. His face was still damp from his morning ritual, and a drop of water fell on my cheek. A vein pulsed in his forehead, but his breathing was slowing down. I felt dirty in his gaze. My hair was a mass of knots, half covering my face, and my sweaty, crumpled nightgown clung to me. No, he surely wasn't worried about me. He doesn't possibly care about *me*. *Me and my mess.*

"If you knew the truth, you wouldn't want me. I'm dirty, and I don't fit into your perfect world. Did you know I was going to marry an Indian when I was old enough? His name was Martin. But then I betrayed him. They all were hanged because of *me*. Every last man in their family. And I watched it all happen. Martin's mom was named *Mary*. Whenever you call me that, you may as well call me a murderer and an adulteress. That's what *she* was."

That much talking wore me out, and the way he had me pinned made it hard to breathe. James gathered me in his arms and talked to me in low tones. He didn't lay me down but rather held me in his arms while he sat down on the bed. He gently combed out my hair with his fingers.

"Well, as I know it, *Mary* has several meanings. Right now, you are Mary, full of rebellion and bitterness. Time will tell if you'll be anything else. You're my wife, and I am committed to you."

I struggled against him—the kinder he was, the more restless I got. "No, I am the bitterbrush, buckbrush, black sage. I'll be your worst enemy. I've never been committed to anyone. Give me time, and I'll leave you, too. You might even hang because of me."

My strength quickly gave out, and I was weak again next to his warmth. James talked softly as he laid me gently down. "The bitterbrush is not my enemy, Mary. It's my helper. Like you'll be . . . My cliff rose . . ."

As I drifted to sleep, I wondered how he could show such kindness to me. Such *hope* in me. Could I be his *cliff rose*? No, he was mistaken about me. But his father said he never made mistakes—he always knew exactly what he wanted. I felt James fix the blanket and leave my side.

In my delirium then, I felt more like the Indian Mary. A drunkard, wailing with regret. Mr. Heins had told me that after the lynchings, Mary's mother would often push her home in a cart from her drinking binges, Mary crying the whole time about her ex-husband and boyfriend Dan. Of course, she didn't cry about Martin. I am just as wretched as she is, I thought.

I was back to wanting to pull my hair out. I was cold, unfaithful, and deceitful. I was self-absorbed and knew nothing of caring for a man. The thought of bearing children even terrified me. I wasn't loving. My children would grow up to be renegades and malcontents, like Frank and Jim. I had a mother who didn't nurture her young. It could be a generational curse. It would be best to get away before there would be any chance of children.

My mind had grown dark, and I was having a hard time remembering anything good. I even started to think negative thoughts about the men in my life. Why hadn't they protected me? My papa had just let my mama dispose of me, like an unwanted leppy calf who had no hope of flourishing. Mr. Heins left me with a complete stranger in Indian territory. Smithy abandoned me by just giving up and dying, even after all his talks of his Maker and an eternal glory. Then there was Henry, who vanished after giving me a glimpse of true life. Compared to this serious James, life with Henry would have been easy. He wouldn't have been so hard on me.

After that last thought of Henry, I strengthened my resolve. Starvation seemed an easy way to die. In all my gloomy years, I had never let my thoughts get this low. I truly was going mad. Where were those words of comfort—of hope? The ones whispered across the desert? I had been forgotten, forsaken. I had been found *unworthy*. Yes—I would refuse all food. He told me he wouldn't force me to eat. James would be relieved. Being such a logical man, he would see it as a disaster avoided.

I could hear James moving around the house, and there were smells of cooking. I saw him sit down at the table with an open Bible in front of him. He had his face in his hands, and I could hear him praying softly. I would just allow sleep to take over before he tried to feed me. That would be an answer to his prayers.

Hunger made it hard to sleep, so I recalled a memory from my journey after Smithy died. It was one of the biggest adventures I ever had—my papa would have loved it. It could have come straight from a western novel, and I often thought of it when I was having trouble sleeping.

Chapter 21
Flesh Upon You
1907

I sat up there behind the buckboard—*alone*, without Smithy—having another episode. My bravery after Smithy died had quickly diminished. I felt panicked, and my breathing was becoming more difficult. I hadn't eaten. I had just given Betty and Crow their heads, and I wasn't even paying attention to where they were going. I continued this way until the sun started going down behind me. I finally gathered that we were heading in a northeasterly direction.

"Thank you, old girls," I told Betty and Crow, and they stared back at me. Did they know they were dealing with one in the throes of hysteria?

They had led me to a small creek and found grass nearby for their supper. This may have been the Badger Creek that Smithy had spoken of with great importance. The horses nodded their heads as they ate and dodged the flies. I didn't even unharness them—I was too lazy, and I wasn't well. I didn't care about eating or even starting a fire. I just rolled up into a ball with the remaining bedding in the back and fell into a dead sleep.

I awoke with flies on my face and was surprised that I had slept so long. The sun was nearly overhead, and Betty and Crow stared back at me with what I saw as disappointment. They must have missed Smithy's cheerful ways, as I did. He would be ashamed to know I had slept in the back of the wagon with the horses harnessed all night. I moved around in the wagon to put things to rights when I heard a disturbing cry.

Before I could make sense of it, the horses bolted. They took off at a dead run, and I fell down in the wagon bed. I looked back and saw the blur of a man on horseback. He chased after us with a horse much faster than Betty and Crow. Betty and Crow were doing their best to get away but had taken us off the beaten path. We bounced over ditches and rocks, and I watched as most of our provisions quickly vanished over the side. Somehow, I managed to crawl back up into the seat to try to gain control of the horses' heads.

It was a hard decision to make. Should I let the horses drive us over a gorge or let myself fall into the hands of the man? I figured the gorge would be bad for all of us, so I tried to slow the horses. Betty and Crow gradually calmed down, and we got back on the tracks. The wagon was almost completely busted apart.

I climbed down and quickly freed the horses from their harnesses. I talked soothingly to them as I had heard Smithy do. I figured I could ride one and pony the other. But then there was the issue of that man headed toward me—at full speed.

He grabbed me up by my arm in one hand and my hair in another. I screamed in pain and fright. He swung me around behind him and managed to grab the horses' ropes all in the same moment. One arm held me while he ponied Betty and Crow with the other. His own mount seemed to know just where to go.

The man was a young Indian, not even twice my age. He was dressed in white man's clothes, which were old but not unclean. He had a rifle slung on his back between us. I could see that he was taking me away from my intended path, and I felt sorry for the pace that Betty and Crow were being forced to keep.

My fear left me weak. Otherwise, you would think I would have attempted an escape. I was in a stupor, thinking of the girls who were kidnapped and killed by angry Modoc women. Would this be my end? A consequence for all my bad feelings toward Mary . . . toward my mother?

After about an hour's ride, we came upon some rock formations, and my captor called out. Two other young men stepped around the rocks and met us with surprised expressions.

"What did you do now, Louie?" one of them asked. I was a little disappointed to hear them talking in English.

A bigger group emerged, including an elderly couple, another man, a young woman, a girl about my age, and a couple toddlers.

"I found a wife," Louie answered as he swung me down before jumping off his horse.

The old woman shook her head and walked over to me. Her husband followed. Although they were all dressed in mostly white man's clothes, the older man had on an Indian headdress. It was a band of buckskin with some feathers at the back.

"Louie, you shouldn't have. She is too young," the woman said.

She gently took my hand and led me around the rock formations to a simple camp. I saw Louie lead Betty and Crow over to their group of horses, where he tied them to a stationary rope. The children were trailing close behind me.

"Are you all right?" she asked me.

I nodded without thinking.

"You are welcome here. We are camping on our journey to find work," she said, pointing in a westerly direction. "They want to find cowboy work."

The men laughed. Louie looked especially happy.

These people did not seem angry or murderous. They were cheerful, in fact. The woman handed me a piece of dried meat and motioned for me to sit. I quietly obeyed and thought things over as I chewed the meat. It must have been my desperation for a *family*, or the comfort I experienced at the Thatchers, that made me momentarily consider going along with Louie's plan. I would *belong*, and I wouldn't have to fall into the hands of another Mrs. Rawlings over in that Denio place. It was just a passing, wild thought, because

Louie was repulsive. He was nothing like my handsome Martin or my vision of the brave Modoc, Captain Jack.

The woman stood up and walked over to the old man. She placed her hand on his arm, "This is my husband." I admired her respect for him.

This made me glance at Louie. He was missing most of his teeth, and his jaw hung loosely open at all times. He maintained a blank stare, and drool dropped off his bottom lip. It looked like he had been in some sort of accident. With that look about him, I was surprised at how fast he had been back there on his horse.

The family seemed very kind, but I had to get away — far away — from Louie. I thought about a plan as the children sat near me, attempting to entertain me with games in the dirt. I kept calm and tried to act agreeable so they wouldn't feel suspicious of me. The old woman smiled and nudged the young woman toward me.

"This is Fawn," she said with a grin.

"Her name is *Fawn*?" I asked.

They all laughed, and the old woman nodded. Fawn walked up, shyly, and began to smooth my hair. It was probably half pulled out of my head after the way Louie grabbed me. Fawn gently combed it with her fingers and tied it back into a braid. She was quietly singing a song in what must have been her native language. She was gentle, and I liked her immediately. She reminded me of Martin's sister, Agnes, with smooth skin and glossy black hair. I wouldn't mind her as a sister, but not if it meant marrying Louie.

The day quickly passed in this easy, peaceful manner. As the sun started to go down, I saw Louie lumber over to his parents. They talked quietly among themselves, and Louie motioned back to me a couple of times, his jaw swaying with each movement. At one point, he walked over and hugged me awkwardly to himself. I stood there stiffly and turned my head away. I tried hard not to vomit.

The old man and his wife shook their heads, and the old woman said, "She's too young. Let's keep her with us, though. She looks like an orphan."

Louie stalked angrily away into the dusk. He was grumbling to himself. The other men were laughing, and even Fawn giggled. She brought a blanket to me and wrapped it around my shoulders. She motioned for me to lie down with her and the children, and I followed along amicably. I carefully examined the layout of the camp one more time before lying down.

If it wasn't for my disturbed thoughts of Louie, I may have fallen into a very comfortable sleep. Fawn was dear, and I was already fond of the little children. I didn't mind sleeping near them. I fought off sleep and watched them drift to sleep through squinted eyelids. I was thankful for a dark night, with just a sliver of a moon.

When I decided everybody must be in a sound sleep, I slowly and quietly moved out of the covers. I pulled the coin from Mr. Heins out of my boot. I left it next to the sleeping Fawn. Maybe it would help feed or clothe the children. My heart was pounding hard, and my breathing must have been loud. Thankfully, our sleeping spot was close to the horses, but every inch felt like a great risk.

My eyes could barely make out the spot where Betty and Crow were tethered. I followed the taut rope to where their halters were tied. The Indians' horses were hobbled. My fingers felt weak as I fumbled with the tight knots. Betty and Crow were both nudging me as if to hurry me along. I started shaking with fear and couldn't untie the knots. It was then that I remembered Mrs. Heins's pretty knife tucked in my boot top. Smithy had said that it was always wise to carry a knife in your boot. If I hadn't done so, the knife might have been part of the debris lost with the wagon.

I fumbled with it and managed to sever both the horses' lead ropes. I didn't have to tell the horses anything—they seemed to know the plan. They were under orders from Smithy to care for me, and I needed to get away from the drooling Louie. I hoisted myself onto Betty's back and pulled Crow alongside. I wanted to see what we could gather from the wagon rubble, and Betty took us in that direction. Nobody in camp had been disturbed.

* * *

I told Maite about this adventure years later, and she said she had heard of a group like theirs living in the desert. They had met a tragic end. A young Indian man had stumbled upon horse thieves and been killed. His family retaliated and killed the horse thieves. A really bad winter followed. I remembered that winter vividly. We had many nights of subzero temperatures. Apparently, with the bad weather, the family had to steal cattle to survive.

Men from over in Cedarville went out to investigate the crime and were killed. It was believed that "Shoshone Mike" or Ondongarte and his family were responsible. A posse was formed, and Ondongarte and his family were ambushed. All were killed except for one girl and three young children.

It was a horrible occurrence and I knew right away that it must have been a different group. I could easily imagine Louie falling into the hands of horse thieves, but I didn't think Fawn's family would have killed those men. I hoped she was doing well and that one day I would see her again. I was thankful to have made a friend—another Indian friend, even. Smithy and Mr. Heins had helped me learn to take a careful look at each individual rather than just compare them all to Mary Hall.

* * *

The desert was silent as I rode on Betty toward the wagon. I felt sad and alone. The sagebrush was all around, but they were not my usual friends. They looked dark, shapeless, and still. Now what? I needed a reason to continue on. I searched the night sky for something familiar, maybe a constellation that Smithy had shown me. I was tired, though, and gave up easily. I leaned forward and hugged Betty's neck. I breathed in her dusty warmth and closed my eyes.

Chapter 22
Cover You
1910

I was conscious enough to know that James, my husband, was trying to feed me. The broth that he made smelled wonderful, and it was a struggle to resist his efforts. I ate a little at a time, forgetting my resolve. When I was fully awake, I was surprised at my feelings. I wanted him to stay next to me. He began talking to me, and I was glad for the escape from my tortured thoughts. His words were poetic, and he gave me a glimpse of the loving nature that Maite had hinted of.

"You can't hide your beauty, my yellow cliff rose. You call yourself *bitterbrush*, but they're one and the same. Without it, my animals wouldn't survive in this desert. They hold steady through the harshness of this land and offer feed even in the cover of snow. The hottest fire won't destroy them. They return with a flourish to sustain. Sweet fragrance beckons, and the life is shared. Just as you attract me, Mary. I want a life with you, a life dependent on our need for each other, the only way to survive in this desert. Please live, Mary. Let me love you! Be like the cliff rose. Don't let those fires win."

James laid his head on me then, and I felt he craved to be near me. The days went by in this fashion. He would pray by my side and even sleep there at times. This rock of a man was letting me see his vulnerability, and I often considered reaching up to stroke his head. But I remained scared. A battle was raging inside, and the fires were threatening. I knew I would fail him and that he would be disappointed in me. I mostly refused the food.

My body was failing, and my mind seemed poisoned. I didn't think I could ever open my heart to love, the love I felt that James was offering me. This wasn't just a fantasy, as I had once imagined with Henry, a love-in-the-escape-from-reality. With James, it would be a story of endurance. Like the twisted trunks clinging and growing ever so slowly—grasping, as the world does its best to kill.

James had fallen asleep with his head against my side. His usually meticulous hair was now falling loose, and I could see the now familiar pulse in his forehead. I had the urge to offer comfort, to nurture. I inched my hand toward him, but memories stopped me short, ones I had never entertained before.

* * *

I had stumbled upon a rare moment when my mother was alone. The house was asleep, but something had beckoned me awake. I was quite young, my hand-me-down gown tickling the tops of my feet as I turned the corner.

She was quietly weeping, her thin frame bent with her head on her arms. When she looked up, I was surprised to see that her usual pinched expression was softened in grief. The tears and weakness looked pretty on her, and I had never seen her that way.

"What is it, Mama?" I was surprised at my boldness.

She drew me down into her lap and curled up tight around me, still weeping.

"I'll never see them again, Mary Cordelia. You'll never know your grandfather and grandmother. They are such good people. Your tall and jovial Uncle Teddy—he can make anyone laugh. And then, your sweet Aunt Rose, always thinking of others. I don't even know how to be good anymore, now that I'm so far away from them. If only your papa could see how much I need them."

"But we can help you, Mama. Papa is so good, too, and I will try to be like Aunt Rose. I'll try to help you more."

"No, Mary Cordelia, you'll never be like her." Mama suddenly pushed me hard off her lap. I fell to the ground. "Go back to bed!"

My mother's angry face changed into another's, just days after the lynchings in Lookout. The streets were full of news reporters, outsiders, and the Law. Mrs. Rawlings's dreams had come true with all the extra business she was getting. Mildred, Sam, and I were hopping to keep up. I knew I was risking punishment, but I just had to get away. I was numb still, avoiding any of those feelings I had tucked away. I wanted to feel something, to think about what I had witnessed.

I sneaked out the back door, longing for my cattle companions. Their owner had moved them to a different pasture. I crawled under the fence and ran across the field. I came to the old cottonwood tree and was surprised to see a lone figure sitting on a rock.

It was Mary Hall, and she was softly keening.

Her shoulders were slumped, as if melting into the rock, and she was swaying.

A brief anger at her presence gave way to pity.

I had an urge to comfort her. I softly touched her shoulder.

"I am sorry about your family, ma'am. You must miss them. I miss Martin . . ."

She lunged at me. I dodged her attempt to grab me.

"Don't touch me, you little wench! I don't want to hear Martin's name in your dirty white mouth."

I felt her spittle on my face. I closed my eyes and spun around. I raced back to the house.

* * *

Those must have been the last times I dared to reach out to comfort someone. I could survive being *unloved*, but I did not want to feel that *rejection* again. The feeling in my heart was so like the chill I had felt on the floor after Mama pushed me down. I had shivered in bed for the remainder of the night, knowing that I could never be a sweet and loveable girl like my long-lost Aunt Rose. Then there was Mary's spittle on my face. I didn't understand. I *had* felt sorry for Mary, not just hatred—but little good did that do. She reviled my attempt to comfort her. Mrs. Rawlings had voiced it clearly—I made people uncomfortable. I was one of the solitary, less colorful plants that Smithy told me about. A weed. I don't know what made James think I could offer any life to him. I think that wind-pollinating plants just die off after a season anyhow. No need for showy flowers, intoxicating aroma, or sweet nectar. *Love* sounded like a lot of effort. And then the *rejection* would come anyhow. I would make a fool of myself.

I lost track of how many days this pattern repeated itself— James's attempts to care for me and my spiraling introspection. It must have been two weeks because Maite was suddenly there.

"Why didn't you come to me, James? How did you let this go on? Oh, sweet girl." Maite was stroking my face.

"She is refusing to eat but a little, Mother. What more could I do?"

"Are you heartless, James? She needs affection and a reason to live! You're probably scaring her to death with all of your fierce ways."

James walked away, looking defeated.

I almost spoke up to defend him then, knowing he had tried to offer those things to me. The problem was all *me*—I was a coward, remember?

"Mary, dear, it is me, Maite. Remember, I told you I'd be here in two weeks? Here I am! I'm going to care for you and get you strong again."

She started by massaging my limbs and applying some sort of musty oil. She sang to me, mostly in her native tongue, but as the day drew on, she sang a hymn or two in English. I endured all of this in a drowsy stupor, but one hymn brought me back with sudden clarity.

"Birds with gladder songs o'er flow,
Flowers with deeper beauties shine,
Since I know, as now I know,
I am His, and He is mine."

Those were my father's words again. Tears flooded down as the song brought me back to those sweet moments with him, years ago.

"Maite? Please . . . sing it again."

Maite's surprised expression at my words turned to recognition. She knew she had found a way into my despair. *A way from my despair.* As she sang hymn after hymn, I began to see that my thoughts were staying in the present and not spiraling downward. When her voice gave out, she hurried to get James and sat him down.

"Sing to her or read to her—anything. She seems to be more alert. I'll add some things to the broth that may stimulate her appetite."

James walked over to my small stack of possessions and rifled through them. I could sense that he was in an agitated mood again.

"Well, this won't help!" He took my Greek mythology book and threw it toward the kitchen. I didn't care.

Then he saw Smithy's Bible and opened the front cover. "Reynold Marks. Is this one of the fellows you almost married?" He asked with a flash in his eye.

I quickly shook my head, afraid he might toss that into the kitchen as well.

"Where did you get it then?"

My throat was sore, but I got the words out. "He was Smithy . . . brought me from Alturas . . . died . . ."

James nodded. "Well, let's read Smithy's Bible then."

James pulled up a chair near my bed and settled in where I could easily watch him. He put up his stockinged feet to where they touched my side. He set his hat askew on his head and opened the Bible. He fixed his gaze on me.

"Do you have a favorite book of the Bible, Mary?"

I quickly shook my head, and he narrowed his gaze. See? He knew that I was a heathen, an imposter.

He cleared his throat and shifted in his chair. "Well, I'm particularly fond of Ecclesiastes. I'll read the twelfth chapter."

I heard Maite sigh from the kitchen.

I had a difficult time following the words at first. I was too distracted by the sight of James and the melodious nature of his voice. I wasn't too scared to stare at him this time since he was looking down. He was beautiful to behold—that glorious thunderhead that catches your eye. He spoke the words with deep reverence, and his expression was earnest.

"Then shall the dust return to the earth as it was: and the spirit shall return unto God who gave it."

This sounded like something Smithy would have said. He had had such a confident, trusting manner when speaking of the things of God. He had been so matter-of-fact. God had made him, and one day he would return to God. Smithy's body was probably still in the process of returning to dust this very moment.

James suddenly looked up and caught me staring at him—he held my gaze.

"This here is a foundational concept, Mary. Everything of this earth is going to come to naught. Only those things we do for our heavenly Father have worth. Those things are eternal."

I closed my eyes and turned my head to the wall. I didn't want him to see my confusion.

He continued reading and then came to the end of the chapter. "'Fear God, and keep his commandments: for this is the whole duty of man. For God shall bring every work into judgment, with every secret thing, whether it be good, or whether it be evil.' Mary? Don't ignore this now."

I had heard him, but I was pretending to be asleep. I was thinking back to my father's heavenly cowboy rescuer at the river. He had told my papa to 'Fear the Lord.' Did Papa do that? Had he lived the rest of his life in some sort of fear? Not that I remembered. He seemed to have more of a simple trust. He may as well have been the one sitting there then, reading to me. The words—so like the ones he had read to me under the tree. They must have been from the Bible, too. The words were a comfort, but I did not understand them. I probably never would, and James and my papa could lament together in their disappointment in me.

"Mary, I know you're listening." James jumped up and got close to my face. I could feel his breath near my ear and smell the bay rum. "Don't turn your face away from me! The way I see it, you're just a selfish young woman. You're in disobedience to the Lord Almighty. Snap out of it! It's time to focus on the here and now--not your troubled past."

"James! What in the world are you saying to her?" Maite said in distress. "I don't know why you're being so forceful . . . And choosing Ecclesiastes, of all the books, to read to her?"

"She's in sin, Mother, and selfish as they come. She's just lying there wallowing in the past and in regrets. I will not tolerate it. We may as well drag her outside and leave her to the fate she desires."

"You are heartless, Son! Go tend to something outside and leave her to me . . . please."

I stole a glance Maite's way and saw her shoving James out with a disgusted expression. James tossed the Bible on my feet with a thud and went out the door.

Maite exhaled deeply and came over to feel my forehead. "I'm so sorry, my dear. I don't always understand him. I think I will read to you something out of First John. You must already know how much God loves you?"

I turned my face to the wall again and kept my eyes closed tight.

Maite cleared her throat and began, "We love him because he first loved us. If a man say, I love God, and hateth his brother, he is a liar: for he that loveth not his brother whom he hath seen, how can he love God whom he hath not seen?"

Her words were just frustrating me. I did not understand how God could love me, and I certainly did not love my brothers. I harbored hatred for them, in fact. So it sounded as if I could never muster up love for God. I wasn't listening anymore as she continued to read about being a child of God. The only thing that was ringing true right then in my ears were James's words:

You are just a selfish young woman . . . focus on here and now.

Chapter 23
Breath in You
1907

Once we had sneaked away from Louie's camp, faithful Betty and Crow led me directly back to the scattered wagon. Louie and his family must have all been fast asleep still. As the light rose in the east, I was energized. I worked quickly, grabbing a handful of items so that I could bridge more distance between myself and that foul man. How foolish of me to only grab the books and a blanket. I gave no thought to sustenance.

It was as if an unseen force were guiding the three of us through the dim light. Betty and Crow must have still been walking in obedience to their kind master. They kept on in a northeasterly direction. I felt alive after our daring escape. The light had dispelled the sadness and loneliness I had felt in the dark. I didn't feel hunger for the first half of that day.

We were covering a lot of ground, and I switched from horse to horse to make sure they wouldn't tire. I was nearly trancelike, looking out around me and swaying with the motion of the horse. Hours went by with me in this state. There was a flower that Chrissy had shown me, and I found myself watching for more of them. She called it Indian paintbrush. I knew the flowers were edible, but I didn't take the time to partake. What caught my interest was the color variety. Back at Nut Mountain, I had only seen dark red flowers. Now I was noticing pink, orange, and nearly white. It looked like the sunrise had laid a blanket across the desert.

If Smithy were with me, he would surely be telling me about the provision of God or His handiwork. Chrissy would have chimed in with the same. I began to talk to Betty and Crow the way they would have.

"Breathtakingly beautiful flowers in a place where I may be the only one to ever see them. Do you ever look at them in wonder, Betty and Crow? Or did God make them purely for His own delight? Maybe they're there to remind us of His presence?"

I was impressed by my own rendition of Smithy's soliloquies. I must have continued like this for quite a while as the sun was directly overhead. The heat beating down on my bare head was my first indication of discomfort. I was suddenly aware of other things, also—hunger, thirst, and exhaustion. I was too lazy, or indifferent, to take any action. Betty and Crow took care of the water situation. They made their way to a small stream that wound around a tabletop mountain. At first, I stayed on Betty's back as she drank, but then I slid off and fell to my knees. I drank deeply, but the cold water only sharpened my hunger. Time was more pressing than my hunger. I still wanted more distance from Louie.

"Ready for me, Crow?" I asked as I slopped myself onto his back.

I had the books tied up in a blanket over my shoulder as I hadn't taken the time to fashion a more sensible way to carry them. This was becoming increasingly uncomfortable, but I was resigned to it. Have you ever heard of a person so helpless . . . or lazy?

My hunger made me feel faint, and I allowed myself to lie down on Crow's neck. I owed him my life many times—both horses, actually. If I started to slip off, my head surely aimed for the nearest rock, Crow would stop and nicker at me. I would center myself again, and in this manner, I occupied the remainder of the day. At one point, I was surprised at some words I recalled, or was it a whispering from across the desert? The words came in time with the horse's steps.

A time to cast away stones, and a time to gather stones together; a time to embrace, and a time to refrain from embracing; a time to get, and a time to lose; a time to keep, and a time to cast away . . .

I could relate very well to the casting away, the refraining, and the losing. At what point would I gather, embrace, or keep? Would I embrace something tangible, physical? As the horses plodded along, I could imagine myself dropping stones, one at a time. That stone was my papa; then the twins and the baby; my confidantes, the cattle; and Martin. Mr. Harden, Mr. Heins, and Mr. Heins's sweet wife were three more stones. Then Pal. Betty and Crow would've loved Pal and Sunny. The Thatchers were cast away and lost, and then dear Smithy. I couldn't leave Fawn out, as I would most likely never see her again, either. My trail of stones faded in the distance behind me.

I remember Smithy promising just a few days' journey left after the Thatcher's. That would mean that I may only have a day between myself and Denio. It seemed that Betty and Crow may have known this in the way they set their faces as flint. I was still ambivalent, not really caring if I lived or died. Just as long as I did not have to live as a wife to drooling Louie. I wondered how many days I could survive without food. Surely quite a few. My father had once told me a story of a cowboy who had been abandoned on the prairie by his spooked horse. I believe it took him close to ten days to drag himself and his broken leg to a place of recuperation. I was absorbed in the melodramatic daydream of Betty and Crow arriving in Denio just after my soul departed to join Smithy. Then Aunt Ruth would have to write Mrs. Rawlings an admonishing letter about how heartless she was to send a young girl on such a perilous journey.

Betty and Crow went around a bend, and I was surprised to see a small structure, similar to Chrissy's house. I slid off my mount and hit the ground with a thud. Both horses stared at me. Did I see pity in their eyes? I spoke to them.

"I'll go in and have a look around. You keep an eye out for Louie."

I pushed open the door and was surprised at the contents of the dwelling. Light filtered through the disturbed dust and revealed a shelf containing a few canned goods. The hunger of my soul still surpassed that of my stomach, however, so I kept looking. I saw what I needed when I turned back toward the door to leave. The wall next to the door was covered with a magnificent painting. It showed a perilous scene that would have left my papa spellbound. It looked like something that would have been described in one his western novels. To see it nearly life-sized, in brilliant color, took my breath away. It showed a wild desert scene with a cowboy whose bronc was determined to lose him. The cowboy was still hanging on to his lasso with which he had successfully entangled the horns of a rangy cow down in a gully. Another cow had gotten tripped up in the rope, and this may have been the last straw for the horse. A couple of other cowboys were not much help as they watched the scene unfold. Cow slobber and dust were flying everywhere. The varied greens of the sagebrush, my kin, were captivating. That cowboy was so brave—*no matter what*, he would not let go of that cow.

"Isn't it beautiful, Papa?" I startled myself. I let the grief wash over me as I stood engulfed in the painting. I sank to the ground and let the tears flow.

"I wish you could see this, Papa. Why do I have to be all alone? Will there ever be someone who won't be taken from me?"

There is a friend that sticketh closer than a brother.

Who?

I was weary of all the words. I didn't understand them. I couldn't see them, and I couldn't touch them. I was so tired of being rejected and alone. I lay on the hard, cold, dirt floor and stared up at the painting. I looked at every inch and noticed down at the corner the name of the man who must have painted it—CM Russell. Next to the name, there was a little sketch of a cow skull. I wonder if he was just a cowboy passing through, or maybe even an Indian. Whoever he was, he should definitely keep painting, I thought.

That painting was the only thing alive for me in that moment. I didn't have a care for what happened next. I lost myself in the vibrant colors and action. I lay there in the dirt and mouse droppings and must have fallen asleep.

I woke up, coughing and spitting out filth. Light entered through the small window and lit up the wild scene for me once again. I thought I could hear the stomping of the animals' hooves, and each exhale and inhale. Then I realize it was just the complaints of Betty and Crow outside. I willed myself to stand up. I considered the canned goods on the shelf but was too depressed to care. I opened the door and caught a whiff of the dewy sagebrush and fresh air. The smell was better than the taste of food, and I could instantly see Smithy before me. He had told me about the power of smell and memory, and I relished the brief glance of him.

"Okay, okay, Betty and Crow. I'll continue on with the plan."

I'll cling to the *plan* like the cowboy did to his catch.

I went back in for one more look at Russell's brilliance. My nose started to run again, and I wiped it with my sleeve.

"Thank you, whoever you are."

I shut the door to protect the little sanctuary and then went and did "eeny, meeny, miny, mo" with Betty and Crow. Betty was the lucky winner this time, and I heaved myself up. The horses continued on toward the rising sun.

The sage seemed to stretch on endlessly, and I wasn't sure I stayed present the whole time. Hunger clenched my insides, and I felt lightheaded. At one point, I leaned over to throw up. Nothing was there but bile.

"Sorry, Betty."

The terrain was rising before me, and we were climbing. The horses picked up speed, and I was surprised to find us now at the top edge of a massive canyon. I panicked and grasped Betty's mane. She had knocked some rocks loose, and they tumbled down, out of sight. I had never seen a gorge so deep and narrow.

"Steady, girl," I managed to say to Betty, louder than I should, backing her away from the cliff.

"*Steady, girl, girl, girl . . .*" the canyon echoed back to me.

I was terrified. I guess I wasn't as ambivalent toward death as I had thought. I held my breath as I backed Betty further away from that gorge. We would have to find a way around it.

"Come on, Crow, keep up. Let's finish this."

We trudged on, and I faded in and out of clarity, nearly tumbling off several times. As darkness closed in, the horses increased their speed even more. They must have sensed we were close. I finally saw lights in the distance, and the horses made their final push. We reached the edge of the little town of Denio, Nevada, and the horses stopped. I suppose they didn't know what business we had come for. I squinted to read the signs on the buildings. There was a blacksmith shop, a store, a schoolhouse, and then I saw it—Ruth's Hotel.

"That makes it easy," I told the horses.

We approached the front of the hotel, and I slid off one last time. I knocked on the door, softly at first, and worked my way up to an impatient banging. Good thing I wasn't half-dead on the horse, I thought. She never would have found me.

Finally, I must have waked her. "I'm coming, I'm coming," Aunt Ruth said, and I heard footsteps. Then I saw her heavy frame approach in the candlelight.

A plump woman, dressed in a mass of white frills, squinted out the window at me.

"Who is it?"

"My name is Corrie, and my papa was your brother. You must be my Aunt Ruth."

Aunt Ruth swung the door open with a flourish and put a hand over her massive bosom.

"Oh mercy, child! Are you all alone?"

"Yes."

I stood stiff as a board as Aunt Ruth awkwardly patted my shoulders.

"You look starved, and you're just filthy! Who is responsible for you?"

Who?

"I guess you are now, Aunt Ruth. All I have is this bundle and these horses."

Aunt Ruth stared at me with a shocked expression and weakly nodded her head. She looked as if she was also thinking of changing her mind.

"Ok, well, I guess we should walk over and wake up old Madge at the Blacksmith's. She'll be able to put up the horses."

I looked over at the horses then. I never saw two more hopeful creatures in my life. They had obeyed their master's command and now would be rewarded with some flaked hay.

Chapter 24
I Am the Lord
1910

Those were all the events that led up to the decision I faced in that small house in Dry Canyon. Would I waste away in my sorrow, or be a wife to James? Would I shrivel from the lack of receiving or giving affection? I suppose my mother faced a similar decision at some point in her life. She didn't starve herself, but she did starve my papa of her love. But then there was Maite, *feeding* her husband . . . and James . . . and me—with love. Could I love like she loves? Could I give of myself that way?

It really was a choice between living and dying. I had been behaving like my own life ended back with those at the bridges. Would I let *life* happen or choose to remain in that *void*? No, it wasn't Henry, or romance, that woke me up. Henry had given me a bit of *otherworldly hope*, sure. But what really brought me to my senses was the realization of my own selfish heart. I had been wallowing in my past, and the Words had exposed the filth.

* * *

I lay there in that bed, in the home that James had offered me, my body weak and my feelings of shame growing ever stronger. I had made my decision, and I sought bravery. Maite had set a pot of soup to simmer and then gone outside to tend flowers. I watched as James came in from his morning chores, shutting the door softly on Maite's pleas. He had his head down. I had the urge to jump up and put my arms around him, but my stubbornness had left me physically weak.

"James!" I called out. He looked over in surprise, and I held out my hands to him. He let go of whatever he was holding and rushed over.

"Mary." He dropped to the side of the bed, and I took his face in my hands.

"I'm sorry . . . I've been selfish . . . so full of self-pity. Can you forgive me?"

I made a feeble attempt to pull him nearer, and he climbed onto the bed next to me.

His face was so close, and his eyes, full of understanding and kindness, held mine. He smelled then like the sage, dirt, and hay, magnified by the morning's warmth. He smiled at me. "Yes, I forgive you. Will you forgive me for my angry outbursts?"

I nodded.

He looked at me as if asking permission before he gathered me to himself. He held me close and then kissed me.

That vulnerability brought freedom—freedom from the prison I had kept myself in. The choice to give unlocked the door. This feeling made me more talkative than ever before.

"I'm starting to understand now, James. Everything my papa said, and you, and the others. About God . . . about *Jesus*. I need to love. *To walk in love.* To be *thankful.* I'm not sure I know how—but I want to try."

James embraced me and whispered, "Mary, my cliff rose . . . Not rebellion and bitterness. You are my *wished-for one* . . ."

The spring rains had been abundant, offering a place for me to die to myself and be raised up alive in Christ. James carried me out the door and straight into the water. Maite walked over, weeping with joy as James faced Heaven and prayed.

"Thank you, Father, for making all things new and for offering life to us who were dead in our sins. This day my wife, Mary Harrison, is a new creation in you and, by your mercy, is born again as your child."

James dipped me under, those cool waters closing over me, and then brought me up, bursting forth into a new life. My tears ran down with the alkali water, and the Living Water, and I was renewed.

Jesus, my Remedy. He made me worthy.

* * *

And that was that. James was so patient and full of grace toward me, and I did my best not to provoke his fiery nature. I loved my dark, fierce husband, and he taught me how to live for Jesus, one day at a time. He gave me countless other gifts—the best ones were our three children. But there was one gift that seemed, at first, a curse—it brought me to my knees.

Our life had been sweet and simple. James and Will cared for the ranches and animals, and Maite and I cared for the homes, the men, and the children. But then World War I came, and with it, Maite's worst fear. James had to leave us and fulfill that destiny of being a leader of men. We missed his vitality when he was gone, and I had to learn to lean on Jesus more than ever. James distinguished himself, of course, and finally returned to us.

I saw James striding toward the house after three years at war and had to steady myself against the doorframe. As he came into focus, I saw that he was pulling a horse, and that horse was pulling a cart. From the cart, he gathered up a bundle and walked toward me.

The bundle was my mama.

James must have seen the life drain from me as I fell to my knees.

"Mary, love, she needs you."

"How, James?" My voice cracked.

It was so like a Nevada rancher to do the hard, right thing.

"There was a letter for us in Denio, and your mother had caught up with it. She was at your Aunt Ruth's. Apparently, no one else will take care of her."

Forsaken . . . alone . . . as I had been . . .

My thoughts were racing. I thought of all my older selfish siblings . . . like her . . . like how I used to be . . . None of them would take her in. I felt so weak and didn't think it would be possible to even speak a word to her.

If a man say, I love God, and hateth his brother, he is a liar.

God had shown compassion to me, and He would help me. He was still reshaping me as His pliable earthen vessel—no longer a brittle pot to be discarded.

I wept as I found the strength to stand and extend my arms toward my James and my mother.

Living through giving.

"I can do it, James. Welcome home, my love. Welcome home, Mama."

Everything grew quiet, as if the world had paused. Mama wanted to say something, and I felt so cold. Would she reject me? What would she say after all the years and miles that had come between us? The last time I saw her, she was casting me out, as one unwanted. She looked up at me, fearfully. Her toothless mouth was sunken in, and she drew her lips in and out with worry. She was awash with sorrow, a shell of a woman. I reached out with a shaking hand and began to stroke her face and hair. Would she push me away like all those years ago? We stood in this manner a while, and then she drew in a deep breath.

It sure was a big breath for one small word, so much it contained. Like the women standing as witnesses at the cross, their hearts breaking with love and sorrow. Beauty in brokenness.

She spoke the word, and I loved it then.

Mary.

Epilogue

So there it is, my sweet girl. Did you hear it, my moment of life? It was in the words, words from across the desert. The Word. I forgot myself in the spoken truth, words bringing life to the dead. Dry bones of pain, guilt, and loneliness were renewed in forgiveness and hope. I had to be a vessel, broken, to be made wholly new. The love of God reached out to me, and I risked it.

For God, who commanded the light to shine out of darkness, hath shined in our hearts, to give the light of the knowledge of the glory of God in the face of Jesus Christ. But we have this treasure in earthen vessels, that the excellency of the power may be of God, and not of us.

Acknowledgements

Please bear with me as I burst with thankfulness . . .

I give thanks "in everything" to my heavenly Father who guides me daily and gently awakened me many mornings to put my thoughts into print;

To eLectio Publishing and to all who have encouraged me in life and this writing process;

To Rachel, Jenni, Leah and Maria, beautifully strong in unique ways, Christ in them, thank you for sticking with me and growing with me, for the priceless laughter;

To all of my friends, precious gifts along this journey;

To Linda Martin, she, along with our children, endured my research getaway. Thank you for your constant interest in the whole process and excellent proofreading. It was so much fun that we will have to do it again! To Debbie Deem, she offered her wisdom, cover art ideas and believed in me. Thank you for faithfully praying for me for at least a decade; To Christine Mohan, she read my book even though she doesn't read fiction. Your art, book, and heart for the victims of trafficking are all admirable;

To those offering fellowship and teaching at Calvary Chapel Red Bluff, Paskenta, Sunrise, the river country up north and midweek, time with you is a precious gift on this earth—more often would be fine with me!

To Cindy Coloma, a lovely, gifted author. Thank you for your many years of encouragement and inspiration.

To Linda Hussa, author and kindred-lover-of-the-desert, you inspired me years ago at your book reading in Reno.

To those sharing the Bend in the river, they literally surround us with friendship and prayer, such Providence!

To Jim and Liz Wills, Jess and Leah Wills, and the rest of our Firestorm Family, God works in amazing ways, and I am so thankful to be a part of your journey; To Paulette Fleming, she took me under her wing all those years ago and showed me the Way; To Marie Neer and Dee Dee Messier, the most challenging and encouraging teachers in high school, they stretched me then, call me Katie and love me still; To Marie, also, for her extensive, priceless guidance with this book. It was such a blessing to rekindle our love for each other over the pages. I felt like a teenager back under your tutelage;

To Shorty and Sharon, they enjoy a good western, thank you for letting me love you;

To our fellow campers-in-remote-desert-places, let's go again!

The most miraculous, squeezable gifts are my family: To Brad and Nancy, thank you for your submission to the Lord and your daily prayers; to Keith and Jennifer, Jared and Sarah, Cody, Devon, Shelby, Akayla, Malachi, Levi, Hannah, Titus, Weston, and Kaitlyn, I love this life with you; to Ron and Sharon, thank you for your gift of time; To Gwen, she dug with me through boxes, and together we discovered Aunt Etta Pepperdine's obituary, I'll never forget that moment in time with you; To our huge, amazing, close family, treasured uncles, aunts, cousins (all those camping trips!), Season and "high fashions," dwellers of the sweetest-cabin-on-earth—who could be more blessed? To Guy, for praying and day-to-day optimism; To Cathy, I love that she calls me her own. Grandma, Dad, Mom, Jake, Will— I still feel the most fortunate;

To my favorite side-by-side sojourners on this earth, Josh, Judge, Kale, and Sarah, you are what He knew I needed. Thank you for your patience as I pursue this dream, and allowing me my "weird introvert" time. I love you.

For Further Enjoyment

Applegate Trail-Leaving High Rock Canyon Marker. California Trail.

Boessenecker, John. *Badge and Buckshot, Lawlessness in Old California*. University of Oklahoma Press. 1988

Bronte, Charlotte. *Jane Eyre*. 1847.

Cox, Tim. *The Lookout Lynching-Murder in Modoc*. 2012

Himmi, Haven. *The Ordeal of Captain Jack* www.prezi.com

Hussa, Linda. *Ride the Silence*. University of Nevada, Reno. 1995

Miller, Joaquin. *As it was in the Beginning*. 1903

Russell, Charles. *A Tight Dally and Loose Latigo*. 1920

Scripture quotations are from the Holy Bible, King James Version. Zondervan. 1995

Smith, Alfred. *Living Hymns*. South Carolina. 1985

Spurgeon, Charles. *The Wordless Book*. 1866

Tell Me a Story. *Artemis and Orion (A Greek Myth)*. www.uexpress.com

The Modoc County Historical Museum, Alturas, CA

The Modoc County Library, Alturas, CA

The Tehama County Library, Red Bluff, CA

Thompson, Colonel William. *Reminiscences of a Pioneer*. www.books-about-california.com

Warren, Kay. *Choose Joy Because Happiness Is Not Enough*. Michigan. 2012

Weigand, Glorianne. *More Dusty Trails*. Oregon. 1996.

CPSIA information can be obtained
at www.ICGtesting.com
Printed in the USA
LVHW112258080419
613464LV00001B/190/P